A SELECTION

The Notebooks
of Joseph Joubert

EDITED AND TRANSLATED BY PAUL AUSTER
WITH AN AFTERWORD BY MAURICE BLANCHOT
North Point Press *San Francisco* *1983*

Contents

vii TRANSLATOR'S PREFACE

1   THE NOTEBOOKS

161 AFTERWORD "Joubert and Space"
     by Maurice Blanchot

Translator's Preface

Joseph Joubert was born in Montignac (Dordogne) on May 7, 1754, the son of master surgeon Jean Joubert. The second of eight surviving children, Joubert completed his local education at the age of fourteen and was then sent to Toulouse to continue his studies. His father hoped that he would pursue a career in the law, but Joubert's interests lay in philosophy and the classics. After graduation, he taught for several years in the school where he had been a student and then returned to Montignac for two years, without professional plans or any apparent ambitions, already suffering from the poor health that would plague him throughout his life.

In May 1778, just after his twenty-fourth birthday, Joubert moved to Paris, where he took up residence at the Hôtel de Bordeaux on the rue des Francs-Bourgeois. He soon became a member of Diderot's circle and from then until Diderot's death in 1784 remained very much under the philosopher's influence. It was through Diderot that Joubert met the sculptor Pigalle and many other artists of the period. During those early years in Paris he also met Fontanes, who would remain his most intimate friend for the rest of his life. Fontanes was several years younger than Joubert, but far more ambitious and easily the most brilliant of the young provincial men who had come to make their way in Paris. Both Joubert and Fontanes frequented the literary salon of the countess Fanny de Beauharnais (whose niece later married Bonaparte); other members included Buffon, La Harpe, and Restif de la Bretonne.

In 1785, Fontanes and Joubert attempted to found a newsletter about Paris literary life for English subscribers, but the venture failed. That same year, Joubert entered into a liaison with the wife of Restif de la Bretonne, Agnès Lebègue, a woman fourteen years his senior. But by March of 1786 the affair had ended—painfully for Joubert. Later that year he made his first visit to the town of Villeneuve and met Victoire Moreau, who would become his wife in 1793. During this period Joubert read much and wrote very little. He studied philosophy, music, and painting, but the various writing projects he embarked upon—an appreciation of Pigalle, an essay on the navigator Cook—were never completed. For the most part, it seems, Joubert watched the world around him, cultivated his friendships, meditated. As time went on, he turned more and more to his notebooks as the place to develop his thoughts and explore his inner life. By the late 1780s and early 1790s, they had become a serious daily enterprise for him.

Joubert had long been a supporter of revolutionary views, and when the Revolution came in 1789 he welcomed it enthusiastically. In late 1790, he was named Justice of the Peace in Montignac, a position that entailed great responsibilities and made him the leading citizen of the town. By all accounts, he fulfilled his tasks with vigilance and fairness and was widely respected for his work. But he soon became disillusioned with the increasingly violent nature of the Revolution. He declined to stand for reelection in 1792 and gradually withdrew from politics.

After his marriage in 1793 he retired to Villeneuve, from then on dividing his time between the country and Paris. Fontanes had gone into exile in London, where he met Chateaubriand. Eventually, upon their return to Paris, Joubert and the two younger men collaborated on the magazine *Mercure de France*. Joubert would later help Chateaubriand with many passages of *Le Génie du Christianisme* and give him financial help in times of trouble. During the early years of the nineteenth century, Joubert was surrounded by many of the most successful men and women in France. Although he lived very much in their shadows publicly, he was deeply admired for his lucid ideas, his insightful critical mind, and above all for his enormous talent for friendship. In 1809, Joubert was named inspector general of education, a post he held for about six years. When he died in 1824 at the age of seventy, Chateaubriand, then Minister of Foreign Affairs, eulogized him in the *Journal des débats*: "He was one of those men you loved for the delicacy of his feelings, the goodness of his soul, the evenness of his temper, the uniqueness of his character, the sharpness and brilliance of his mind—a mind that was interested in everything and understood everything. No one has ever forgotten himself so thoroughly and been so concerned with the welfare of others. . . ."

Although Fontanes and Chateaubriand had both urged Joubert to put together a book drawn from his daily writings, the notebooks remained unpublished during his lifetime. The first selection to appear in print, entitled *Pensées*, was compiled by Chateaubriand in 1838. Exactly one hundred years later, the complete notebooks were published in two volumes by Gallimard (*Les Carnets de Joseph Joubert*), edited by André Beaunier); I have used the Gallimard edition in making my selections for this book.

Excluding his correspondence and the aborted writings of his youth, the 900 tightly printed pages of the two Gallimard volumes represent Joubert's entire output as a writer. Joubert was not a writer of maxims in the traditional French manner. He was something far more difficult to define: a writer who spent his whole life preparing himself for a work that never came to be written, a writer of the first order who paradoxically never managed to produce a book. The numerous reflections on writing to be found in the notebooks take their place alongside Joubert's daily preoccupations and are scattered among his observations on the weather, the landscape, family, society, and politics. "These thoughts form not only the foundation of my work, but of my life."

No more than a tenth of that work is contained in this volume. In choosing the entries, I have been guided above all by my own contemporary and idiosyncratic tastes, concentrating my attention on Joubert's aesthetic theories, his "imaginary physics," and passages of direct autobiographical significance. I have not included the lengthy reading notes Joubert compiled during his study of various philosophers—Malebranche, Kant, Locke, and others—nor the frequent references to writers of his time, most of whom are unknown to us. For convenience and economy, I have eliminated the dates that precede each entry.

I first discovered Joubert's work eleven years ago, through an essay by Maurice Blanchot. In it, Blanchot compares Joubert to Mallarmé and makes a solid case for considering him as the most *modern* writer of his period, the one who speaks most directly to us now. Nothing written on Joubert, it seems to me, could serve as a better accompaniment to this book.

P.A.

New York; April 30, 1982

The Notebooks

1783 (?)

The only way to have friends is to throw everything out the window, to keep your door unlocked, and never to know where you will be sleeping at night.

You will tell me there are few people mad enough to act like this. Well then, they shouldn't complain about not having any friends. They don't want any.

___

Do you want to know how thought functions, to know its effects? Read the poets. Do you want to know about morality, about politics? Read the poets. What pleases you in them, deepen: it is the truth.

___

In order to write perfectly, one must write and think in the same way a perfect man would write and think at the moment when all the faculties of his being were in perfect harmony. This situation would be possible in some state of soul in which all the passions were developed in all their force and to their full extent and combined in perfect equilibrium.

___

It is up to poets to form languages and up to philosophers to reform them. How many words are wrong! And if the accumulation of discoveries each generation must pass on to the next were as vast as it could be, every language would undergo a revolution every hundred years.

——

In France we seem to like the arts more to judge them than to enjoy them.

——

I am trying to figure out what place women should occupy in the republic. We have made a sort of property out of them. Is this dominion just? I remind myself of the principle I established earlier: "whenever an institution destroys a single right of a single person, this institution is bad."

——

Men are children. They must be pardoned for everything, except malice.

——

During the rain there is a certain darkness that stretches out all objects. Beyond that, its effect on our body forces us to withdraw into ourselves, and this inwardness makes our soul infinitely more sensitive. The very noise rain produces, which the Latins called *densissimus imber*, continuously occupies the ear, awakes attentiveness and keeps us on the alert. The brownish hue the moisture gives to the walls, the trees, the rocks, adds to the impression these objects make. And the solitude and silence it spreads out around the traveler, by forcing animals and men to be quiet and to seek shelter, makes these impressions more distinct. Enveloped in his coat, his head covered, and moving along deserted paths, the traveler is struck by everything, and everything is enlarged before his imagination or his eyes. The streams are swollen, the grass is thicker, the stones are more sharply defined; the sky is closer to the earth, and all objects, closed up in this narrowed horizon, occupy a greater space and importance.

———

What makes the waters consoling is their movement and their limpidity. . . .

———

When a nation gives birth to an individual capable of producing a great thought, another is born who is capable of understanding and admiring it.

———

If I die and leave several scattered thoughts on important things, I beg in the name of humanity that those who see what has been left suppress nothing that seems at odds with accepted ideas. During my life I loved only the truth. I feel I have seen it in many great things. Perhaps one of these [words?] that I have dashed off in haste . . .

1784

If the earth must perish, then astronomy is our only consolation.

1785

I imitate the dove, and often I throw a blade of grass to the drowning ant.

1786

O my friends! I have drunk love . . .
   Nota. Socrates had observed (*sic*) that to taste wines
properly we must sip them while drinking. A lesson of
pleasure and temperance! . . .

———

If curiosity had not made us examine the nature of plants,
how they take root, how they grow, how they die, how
they reproduce . . . we would enjoy their fruits no more
fully than animals do, and perhaps with even less pleasure. . . .

———

If there is one sad thing in the world, it is the poplar on the
mountains. . . .

———

Every sound in music must have an echo; every figure must
have a sky in painting; and we who sing with thoughts and
paint with words, every sentence and each word in our
writings must also have its horizon and its echo.

———

Thought forms in the soul in the same way clouds form in
the air.

1787

A work of genius, whether poetic or didactic, is too long if it cannot be read in one day.

——

Apparent extension of the fields on Sunday. Born of two causes: absence of sounds and absence of visible objects.

Noise that comes from a single place makes the places around it seem deserted. When it comes from several, it makes even the intervals seem populated.

It is to the mind, to the soul even more than to the eye, that the countryside seems extended, immense, uninhabited.

——

The silence of the fields. How everything hushes imperceptibly with the fall of night. How everything seems to be gathered up: men and animals, by the work of unanimous silence; plants and all things that move, for the wind falls when evening comes near, and the air holds only a single, frail breath. It is from this immobility of all things, and because the remaining light is reflected more during these tranquil hours by the earth and its rocks than by the trees and plants, that the hills and fields seem to lift up the earth and to stand in wonder.

——

9

Sad harvests . . .

———

The essential thing is not that there be many truths in a work, but that no truth be abused.

1789

——There is no more white paper on the earth and the source of ink has dried up.——Give my pen an iron point, a diamond point, give me leaves of copper; I will engrave on them. . . .——

——

It is not facts, but rumors that cause emotions among the people. What is believed creates everything.

Extension is the body of God, as Newton would readily say.

——

Mixture of dry and wet. Water swells before boiling.

1790

The ears and eyes are the doors and windows of the soul.

———

. . . And travel through open spaces where one sees nothing but light . . . *Like Plato.*

———

. . . They are born old . . .

1791

Inundation. The Seine wanted to see the Bastille destroyed. It invoked the waters of heaven, and the waters of heaven carried it to the foot of the walls, where those famous towers once reigned, and which the inhabitants of Paris leveled to the ground three times three months and nine days ago.

———

Are you listening to the ones who keep quiet?

———

A winter without cold and without fire.

———

Always to link unknown things to known things.

———

The republic is the only cure for the ills of the monarchy, and the monarchy is the only cure for the ills of the republic.

———

———. . . where the accusers are almost always the guilty ones.

———

The reading of Plato is like mountain air. It does not nourish, but it sharpens our faculties and gives us a taste for fine food.

———

Through memory we travel against time, through forgetfulness we follow its course.

———

In these times of trouble, one commits and suffers great evil.

———

Everything that has wings is beyond the reach of the laws.

———

———*Nota.* We must do as much to read an abbreviation as to read a word written in its entirety. This is because it is the mind that reads and not simply the eyes.

———

We are in the world as words are in a book. Each generation is like a line, a phrase.

———

Writing is closer to thinking than to speaking.

———

The cock sings the hours. It has sung midnight.

1793

Wisdom is the strength of the weak.

———

His ink has the colors of the rainbow.

———

Let heaven forgive the wicked, after they have been punished.

———

In order to live, we need little life. In order to love, we need much.

———

It is necessary that something be sacred.

———

The good is worth more than the best.

———

What makes civil wars more murderous than other wars is that we can more easily accept having a stranger for an enemy than a neighbor; we do not want to keep the possibility of vengeance so near.

———

A sluggish river that carries nothing.

——

Imitate time. It destroys slowly. It eats away, it uses up, it uproots, it detaches and does not rip apart.

——

In their words one hears the tinkling of their brains.

——

We need a ladder to the mind. A ladder and rungs.

1794

Here is the desert. In this silence everything speaks to me: and in your noise everything falls silent.

———

Freedom. That is to say, independence of one's body.

———

The number of books is infinite.

———

***My son was born during the night of the 8th and 9th, at two and a quarter hours past midnight.
That he one day remember the pains of his mother!

———

***we gave the child his names. It was the wise woman who named him, beside the fire, at three o'clock in the afternoon.
He is named *Victor Joseph*, after his mother and myself.
That same day I heard the nightingale.

———

I thought of my own happiness, of the mother's calm and peace in body and soul, of the fine and decent shape of the child, which is an inestimable good. Though born of a weak mother he is quite strong. His constitution is healthy.

17

He came into this world at Lacédémone. The child and
mother are doing well. After so many fears concerning
them both, such happily demented fears, I told myself *rejoice*.

————

I stayed at home and walked in the little garden to be alone
in my joy.
     Labor was never happier, nursing never less difficult.
The child does not seem wicked.

————

***The gray bird
in the Chaumont woods.

————

The mother got out of bed. Her thinness is considerable.
The child nursed the whole time she was carrying him.
     Today he opened his eyes more often and longer than
usual. He even seemed to want to smile when his aunt tick-
led him.

————

Of the last word.—The last word must be the last. It is like a
last hand that puts the last nuance on a color, nothing can be
added to it.
     Nuance on nuance—in this way color is formed.
     Transparency on transparency.

————

Big words. Claim too much attention.

————

Eye—is the sun of the face.

———

The sieve of forgetfulness. Or the riddle of forgetfulness.
Or: Memory and forgetfulness are the mother and
father of the muses. True knowledge is composed of these
two things. Or: it holds a riddle in its hand. This riddle is
called forgetfulness.

———

The soul paints itself in our machines.

———

Tragedy and marionettes. The strings. Undoing the
strings. The ropes.

———

All truths are double or doubled, or they all have a front and
a back.

———

Soul.—It is a lit vapor that burns without consuming itself.
Our body is its lantern. Etc. The flame of this vapor is not
only light but feeling. Etc.

———

I have little sap. Etc.

———

They cannot accustom themselves to lacking nothing.

———

Prescience. Is it possible?

1795

Children must have stories.
    Children: who cannot speak. In talking to them, we soften our voice. We lower its volume, its range, etc.

——

The sun is clipped. Fogs.
Nota. Hair, like rays.
Fogs that dust the trees.

——

Roundness. This shape guarantees matter a long life. Time does not know where to take hold of it.

——

These *coups d'état* are necessary, you tell me. I answer you, what is sinister and criminal is never necessary at any time.

——

One writes with a pen, the other writes with a brush.

——

Children always want to look behind mirrors.

——

Imitate the spinner. Imitate the ant. One gathers during the summer what is necessary in winter, and the other prepares in winter what is necessary in summer.

—

Nimbleness. Agility of mind. These works are no more than perilous leaps into space.

—

Dreams. Their lantern is magical.

—

Love and fear. Everything the father of a family says must inspire one or the other.

—

Light. It is a fire that does not burn.

—

A tact placed before us and outside us.—An inner tact.

1796

The ancients knew about anatomy only through war. It was on the battlefields that they learned all they knew about it.

———

The splendor of fire. The word *clangor* for sound answers that of *splendor* for light.

———

In these times when minds are not calm.

———

Twenty-five-thousand-four-hundred-sixty-nine laws! . . .

———

The beauties of transition and those of isolation.

———

Passions come like a smallpox and disfigure this original beauty.

———

The people. They know how to know, but not how to choose.

———

He must confess his darknesses.

———

I will build a temple for the worship of dreams.

———

Give me a morality that equally suits the healthy and the sick, men and women, children, adults, and old people.

———

Everything that cannot grow diminishes, even the qualities that are passed on. Is this true?

———

An age in which we have children who can scarcely remember having seen their fathers.

———

The first part and last part of human life are what is best about it, or at least what is most respectable. The one is the age of innocence, the other is the age of reason. You must write for these two ages and banish from your mind and your books that which does not suit one or the other.

———

I love to see two truths at the same time. Every good comparison gives the mind this advantage.

———

. . . His necessity invincibly proves his existence.

———

Illusion is in sensations. Error is in judgments. We can know truth and at the same time take pleasure in illusion.

———

One loves to say what he knows, and the other to say what he thinks.

———

Pleasures are always children, pains always have wrinkles.

———

The imagination is the eye of the soul.

———

There are truths that cannot be apprehended in conversation.

———

Forbidden to speak of God . . .

———

What comes through war is given back through war. All spoils will be retaken, all plunder will be dispersed. All victors will be defeated and every city filled with prey will be sacked in its turn.

———

With the telescope, with the microscope, we have seen a great number of phenomena; and that is all.

———

Plato. He is an author whose ideas cannot be understood until they have become our own.

———

Take us back to the time when wine was invented. . . .

———

The penchant for destruction is one of the ways used for conserving the world.

———

Divorce. Its existence and use should be determined only by the interests of the children.

———

We must give reasons to people that are not only good for us but good for them as well.

———

The hordes of words that fill our books proclaim our ignorance, reveal the obscurities that flood our knowledge. If we were perfectly enlightened, our moral books would contain only maxims and our books on physics and spirituality would contain only axioms and facts. Everything else is clutter and shows no more than our gropings, our effforts, and our difficulties.

———

Deism. The human species cannot accommodate itself to it. This doctrine relates to our strengths but not to our weaknesses.

———

Illusion is an integral part of reality. It is an essential presence, in the same way an effect is essential to a cause. (Integral part, which means a part without which a thing does not have the whole integrity of its constitution or application, etc.)

———

Fathers love their children because they are theirs. The more a child becomes the property of his father through the law, the more he will be loved. For the happiness of the children themselves paternal authority must be given great scope and weight.

Nevertheless, a child should not be his father's thing, as Diderot understood it, but he should be his person, in brief, he should belong to him to the extent that one human being can belong to another.

———

Models.—There are no more models.

———

When a thought gives birth to obscurity, it must be rejected, renounced, abandoned.

———

God is the place where I do not remember the rest.

1797

In order to be known, he would have to make us immortal and give us another life.

———

There is a class of society in which pious children do not know their parents are mortal. They have never dared to think about it.

———

We cannot imagine the *all* as having form, for every form is but the visible and palpable difference of the object that is clothed by it.

———

To compensate absence with memory.

———

A flower that cannot bloom, a bud that cannot open.

———

To seek wisdom rather than truth. It is more within our grasp.

———

Chance is a role that providence has reserved for itself in the affairs of the world, a role through which it could make certain that men would feel they have no influence.

———

Anger makes us adroit.

———

Democracy and slavery inseparable. Why. Democracy as it existed among the ancients was no more than government by a number of men large enough to be called the people. But this designation is false. The true people, in such a state, the greatest number, the majority belong to the class of slaves, and slavery inevitably develops in a country governed in this way, because it is impossible that those who spend their time making laws can make shoes and clothes, plant crops, work fields, etc.

———

The mind can only create errors. Truths are not created, they exist; one can only see them, disentangle them, discover them, and expose them.

———

Lovers. Whoever does not have their weaknesses cannot have their strengths.

———

Clarity of mind is not given in all centuries.

———

We do not write our books in advance, we do them as we write them. What is best about our works is hidden by scaffoldings: our texts are filled with what must be kept and what must be left behind.

————

They do not know how to apply names to things.

————

Forgetfulness of all earthly things, desire for heavenly things, immunity from all intensity and all disquiet, from all cares and all worries, from all trouble and all effort, the plenitude of life without agitation. The delights of feeling without the work of thought. The ravishments of ecstasy without medication. In a word, the happiness of pure spirituality in the heart of the world and amidst the tumult of the senses. It is no more than the gladness of an hour, a minute, an instant. But this instant, this minute of piety spreads its sweetness over our months and our years.

————

Yes, the soul must breathe. This wave is its air, its space. Within it, it can move at will. A single bit (*haustus*) of this element is enough to refresh, it contains the principle of its well-being—which is the effect of its moderations.

————

In metaphysics, the art of writing consists of making sensible and palpable what is abstract. To make abstract what is palpable is its vice and fault. It is the fault of those we have so mistakenly called metaphysicians in this century.

————

We have the memory of individuals, but we do not have the idea. We have the idea of qualities and cannot have a mem-

ory of them. Memory is the representation of fixed and determined figures. The idea cannot . . .

————

What our eyes see, our imagination can no longer see. The
same things cannot be the object of both kinds of seeing.

————

For our entire lives we are for moral things what children
are for physical things, wanting to join enormously dispro-
portionate things to each other, to adjust big clothes to little
bodies and long shoes to little feet.

————

A sensibility that overflows; that is to say, it spreads beyond
its canal and is not held back by the dikes of reason. It floods
all objects and fills the head as well as the heart.

————

Perfection is composed of minute things. It is ridiculous to
put them aside and not to use them.

————

The exclusive study of natural history bends us constantly
toward the earth. The mind no longer lifts its eyes.

————

The imagination has made more discoveries than the eye.

————

Psalms. Read them with the intention of praying and you
will find them beautiful. Eh! Doesn't every reading demand
a readiness of mind that is special and appropriate to it?

————

Life is born in the same way as fire, from friction. Moisture and fire are not incompatible.

Life spreads into all places. All space is filled with it.

Like fire, it is kindled, it flares, and is fixed by being joined to the individual, like fire when it consumes a candle.

———

Why do I get so tired when I speak? Because, when I speak, a part of my strength is exerting itself while the other part is inactive; the part that is acting alone supports the difficulty and the weight of the action and is soon overwhelmed. This unequal distribution of forces in me leads to an unequal distribution of activity in all my parts. Therefore: total fatigue when the strong part is fatigued, because then the weakness is everywhere.

———

When men are imbeciles, the one who is mad dominates the others.

———

The tomb swallows us, but it does not digest us. We are consumed but not destroyed.

———

God made life to be lived (the world to be inhabited) and not to be known.

———

The thoughts about which we can say: "There is rest in this thought." This image is encouraging.

———

This world seems to me a whirlwind inhabited by a people
whose head keeps turning and turning.

———

The dying inherit the dead.

———

Imprisoned in our body . . . and our soul has its windows.

———

Don't cut what you can untie.

———

Sacred language. It should be hieroglyphical. All words
should seem hollowed out or in relief, chiseled or sculpted.
Black and white, emptiness and fullness are suitable to it.
Everything must be juxtaposed and united, but separated
by intervals.

———

The intellectual world is always the same. It is just as easy to
know it today as it was in the beginning, and it was just as
hidden in the beginning as it is today.

———

To create the world, a speck of matter was enough, for
everything we see, this mass that frightens us, is no more
than a speck that eternity has set in motion. Through its
malleability, through the hollows it closes up and the art of
the worker who did the work, this speck offers a kind of
immensity in the embellishments that emerge from it. A
speck of gold will explain us, etc.

———

Everything seems full to us; everything is empty, or, to be more exact, everything is hollow.—Everything is hollow; and the elements themselves are hollow. God alone is full.
   —Penetrable bodies are more hollow than the others.

———

"Yes, please cut up the pieces for me," he said, "but don't chew them."

———

It is a drop of breathed water, a speck of flattened metal.

———

Thought is not a greater marvel than thinking. Nor, perhaps, does it demand an immateriality that is any purer. Both operate through representations made by the inner mirrors that our inner sight is constantly looking into.

———

Do not say the word that completes the symmetry of your sentence and rounds it off when the reader will inevitably think of it and say it to himself after having read the words that precede it.

———

Intimate interior evidence. Clarity without any flash. Built by the ease of belief. The *invidence*, if such a word can be used.

———

Our arms are canes of flesh with which the soul reaches and touches.

———

In a grain of sand there is fire, water, air, and dust.

————

The air itself is only the body of another, far more subtle air.
  To change my diamonds into pearls . . .

————

The weakness of the dying slanders life.

————

Do not: —Define what is known: gossip. Obscure what is clear: scribbling. Question what exists: bad faith, ignorance. Make abstract what is palpable: charlatanism. Present difficulties that are not there or are only apparent: deceit.

————

Tell me what is happening on earth.

————

All these philosophers are no more than surgeons.

————

Resignation is a hundred times easier than courage, for it has a motive outside of us and courage does not. If both diminish evils, let us use the one that diminishes it the most. (Outside us, that is to say beyond our will.)

————

Remember to let your ink grow ripe.

————

The shifting path of the waters . . .
A river of air and light . . .
Folds of clarity . . .

————

Sexes. One has the look of a wound, the other of something skinned.

———

Matter is a part of itself that is beyond itself.

———

Where do thoughts go? Into the memory of God.

———

Beautiful enclosures please us because they clearly print in us the idea of a portion of space; just as a beautiful harmony makes us feel spontaneously and unconsciously the movement and repose that are the elements of time.

———

God's light goes to the stars and from the stars to us.

———

Delicate minds are all sublimely born minds that have not been able to take flight, because of weak organs, or erratic health, or because lazy habits have held them back.

———

The world was populated by artists who limited themselves to painting society as they found it and let everything stay as it was, whether beautiful or flawed. They are followed by true masons who want to rebuild it.

———

The staircase that leads us to God. What does it matter if it is make-believe, if we really climb it? What difference does it make who builds it, or if it is made of marble or wood, of brick, stone, or mud? The essential thing is that it be solid and that in climbing it we feel the peace that is inaccessible to those who do not climb it.

——

Around every flame there must be a void, so there can be light. Without space, no light.

1798

What is a diamond, if not a bit of gleaming mud?

———

One can be stingy with words, but not stingy with syllables.

———

Nothing is perfect on this earth. Even piety is imperfect.
Even the piety of saints.

———

Images have had a great influence on realities.

———

The sign then makes us forget the thing signified.

———

What good is modesty?—It makes us seem more beautiful
when we are beautiful, and less ugly when we are ugly.

———

Beauties that leave nothing to the imagination.

———

To hide our eyes to make others believe we are hiding tears.

———

The truth. They make it consist of nothing they cannot
prove. The greatest happiness they find in it is being able to
put forward incontestable assertions. This is what they like,
and they consider it a sign of prestige, a prerogative, a
power, a dignity, etc., a liberation from error.

———

Illusion. God created it and placed it between the seeds,
the fruits, flesh, and the palace of the mouth, and from this
tastes were born; between the flowers and their smells, and
from this perfumes were born; between hearing and
sounds, and from this was born harmony, melody, etc.,
between the eyes and objects, and from this were born
colors, perspective, beauty.

It is a small bit of nature that amuses itself by giving us
pleasure through evaporation.

It is different from error. If I see colors without seeing
any object, as in the air for example, I am in error. In the op-
posite case, I am under an illusion and still within the truth.

All illusion is produced by some emanation and is the
effect of a cloud, a vapor, the intervention of a fluid. If the
organ is tainted, if the object is improperly disposed or al-
tered in its constituent parts, there is no illusion. One of the
two parts is then lacking to set the process in motion, and
the play of illusion can no longer work.

Illusions. They can thus be produced only by these ef-
fluvia, these invisible outflows, these subtle emanations that
maintain the perpetual currents between these different
beings. They cannot therefore give and receive agreeable
sensations if they do not somewhere produce some loss of
substance. Thus, to the condition of change and decline is
attached the good of inspiring and feeling pleasure.

———

The breath of God. God created everything with his breath.

———

Nothing in the moral world is lost, just as nothing in the material world is annihilated. All our feelings and thoughts on this earth are only the beginnings of feelings and thoughts that will be completed elsewhere.

———

The only good in man is his young feelings and his old thoughts.

———

Stars more beautiful to the eye than to the telescope that robs them of their illusions.

———

Music, perspective, architecture, etc. Embroider time, embroider space.

———

To draw up in advance an exact and detailed plan is to deprive our mind of the pleasures of the encounter and the novelty that comes from executing the work. It is to make the execution insipid for us and consequently impossible in works that depend on enthusiasm and imagination. Such a plan is itself a half-work. It must be left imperfect if we want to please ourselves. We must say it cannot be finished. In fact it must not be, for a very good reason: it is impossible. We can, however, draw up such plans for works whose execution and accomplishment are a mechanical thing, a thing that depends above all on the hand. This is suitable and even very useful for painters, for sculptors. Their senses, with each stroke of the brush or chisel, will find this novelty that did not exist for their minds. Forms and colors, which the imagination cannot represent to us as perfectly as the eye can, will offer the artist a horde of these encounters which are indispensable to giving genius pleasure in work. But the orator, the poet, and the philosopher will not find the same encouragement in writing down what they have already thought. Everything is one for them. Because the words they use have beauty only for the mind and, having been spoken in their head in the same way they are written on the page, the mind no longer has anything to discover in what it wants to say. A plan however is necessary, but a plan that is vague, that has not been pinned down. We must above all have a notion of the beginning, the end, and the middle of our work. That is to say, we must choose its pitch and range, its pauses, and its objectives. The first word must give the color, the beginning determines the tone; the middle rules the measure, the time, the space, the proportions.

———

. . . This spark that unexpectedly fell on my childhood and burned my entire youth.

———

In the same way that man was made in the image of God, the earth was made in the image of heaven.

———

. . . Pleasure of being seen from afar.

———

A century in which the body has become subtle, in which the mind has become coarse.

———

One fills himself only with juices, warm waters, vapors, lightnesses. The other concerns himself only with matter, animals, minerals, configurations, and weights. Bodies that receive an over-subtle nourishment and minds concerned only with objects that are too real and too hard, are equally depraved.

They have an earthly mind with airy bodies.

———

To live without sky . . .

———

To reason, to argue. It is to walk with crutches in search of the truth. We come to it with a leap. We must use reasoning to make sure we have reached the end and that we have covered the whole path. Likewise in the stadium, the runner touches the stone with his hands and steps back to see the barrier in front of the goal.

These false rules only serve to persuade those who observe them that they have attained what they cannot attain.

We have led our minds astray. . . .

———

Among the three extensions, we must include time, space, and silence. Space is in time, silence is in space.

———

To be in one's place, to be at one's post, to be part of the order, to be content. Not to murmur of suffering, to be incapable of being unhappy.

———

Too much talk (they say). *Nota bene*: too much writing.

———

It is impossible to love the same person twice.

———

That peace is the object of morality and politics. Peace with oneself, peace between citizens, peace between the city and strangers.

———

This life: the cradle of our existence.— What do they matter then—sickness, time, old age, death—which are merely the various degrees of a metamorphosis that perhaps only begins here on earth. Alas! these clarities escape us! and this is one of the insurmountable fatalities of our present lot. I would like to be able to remember, however, in that far-distant future, all the fugitive moments of my present life which by then will have been in the eternal past for such a long time. The ones who will be happiest are those who will not have a single moment from their lives that cannot be represented distinctly and with pleasure in memory.— There as here our memories (which will be sharp) will make up the better part of what is good and bad in us. This very moment that I am speaking to you, this moment in which I am saying this, will be repeated forever. Man lets time get lost, but there are no lost moments.

———

The cry of the chimney sweep; the song of the cricket.

———

Strength without repose (in Lavater).— Forces always at work, an activity without rest, movement without intervals, agitation without calm, passions without melancholy, pleasures without tranquility. It is to live without ever sitting down, to grow old standing up, to banish slumber from life and to die without ever having slept.

———

To think what we do not feel is to lie to ourselves, in the same way that we lie to others when we say what we do not think. Everything we think must be thought with our entire being, body and soul.

———

Desire to be a bird, desire to become a bee. Man feels that his happiness is in the air.— And if we wish to become a bird, it is not an eagle, a vulture, a pheasant, a partridge, or a parrot that we wish to become, but a modest little bird gifted with amiability, a warbler, a titmouse, a robin, a nightingale, an average and innocent bird. For neither do we wish to become a hummingbird.

———

Always to explain the moral world by the physical world is not necessarily a good idea. For in the physical world we often take appearances for realities and our conjectures for facts. We thus risk making two errors instead of one by applying to one world the false dimensions we give to the other. Applications of the moral world to the political world are more appropriate.

———

Shadows on the wall: judgments, conjectures.

———

Everything is double and is made up of a soul and a body. The universe is the body of God (but here the body is in the soul). The mind's body is matter. There is the body of the body. The body of the rarefied is the dense, and the hard is the body of the dense. Always and endlessly, the thick and the thin hold to the inner and the outer. Everything is made of more and less. No body without soul, no soul without

body. If there is the body of the body, there is perhaps also
the soul of the soul.

Nota. How it happens that in searching for words we
come to ideas. Words are the bodies of thoughts.

————

(For the child.)
Does he speak?—No, he does not speak to us, but he hears
us.—Did he make this tree?—No, but he made the first tree,
and all the others have come from it.

In heaven there is a great book. Everything we say, do,
and think is written in it.—In what language?—God
knows, but we do not know. Yes, what we are saying now,
what we will say today, and all that we can say for as long as
our life lasts.

Can we see him?—We can see him with our mind.—
Why not in another way?—Because our eyes prevent it.
God does not have a body like ours: that is why we cannot
see him when we have a body. He gave us his idea . . . We
will know him when we are in heaven . . . A child cannot
know what a man knows, a man cannot know what an angel knows, an angel cannot know what God knows.

————

Sometimes, in order for a thing to be used, what is superfluous is essential. Thus the flesh of a pear is worth more to us
than its seeds, even though for its reproduction, which is the
great goal of nature, the seed is what is necessary, sufficient
unto itself, and the flesh is what is superfluous, too much.

————

The style is the thought itself.

————

How, when languages are formed, ease of expression is
harmful to the mind, for no obstacle thwarts it, contains it,

makes it cautious, or forces it to choose among its thoughts,
a choice it is forced to make in languages that are still new,
by the delay that requires it to look for its words and to
search through its memory. In this case one can write only
with great attention.

———

Every body is no more than a film (I speak of bodies that
move and that have a soul within them). All depth is only a
point. All weight is the weight of a straw, a particle of
feather . . . even less.

———

J.-J. Rousseau. In his books we learn how to be discon-
tented with everything outside of ourselves.

———

God. It would not be bad to represent him through perfumes and light, with light at the center.

This life, which holds our soul in the cradle, if I can express myself in this way. It surrounds the mind with swad-
dling clothes and covers it with obscurities.

———

Passions. The ancients called them *troubles*; and rightly so:
why.

———

Beyond bodies, beyond worlds, beyond everything,—beyond and around bodies, beyond and around worlds, beyond and around everything, there is light and there is
mind. Without mind, I mean the elemental mind, everything would be full and nothing would be penetrable; there
would be no movement, no circulation, no life.

———

When children ask for an explanation, and we give it to
them and they do not understand it, they are still satisfied
and their minds have been put at rest. And yet what have
they learned? They have learned that what they no longer
wish not to know is very difficult to know, and in itself this
is a kind of knowledge. They wait, they are patient, and
with reason.

———

Memory.—It is a mirror that retains, and retains forever.
Nothing is lost in it, nothing is erased. But it can be tar-
nished. And then one sees nothing in it.

———

J.-J. Rousseau. Of the power of words. Of their heat.
Warm words. This style that makes us feel its flesh and
blood.

———

The memory of death: is it not able to maintain in us the
natural compassion we have for suffering?—And this death,
this childhood, etc.

———

Newton. It is no more true that he has discovered the system of the world than it is true that someone who balances
the accounts of an administration has discovered a system
of government.

———

Beautiful clothes are a sign of joy.

———

The skies of skies, the sky of the sky.

1799

Like Daedalus, I am forging myself wings. I construct them little by little, adding one feather each day.

———

Illusion or play. Everything agreeable is in them.

———

When men lose their childishness, that readiness of childhood to fear and honor powers that are invisible, when an excessive mental audacity puts them above all belief, then they have left the sphere of the accustomed order, they have passed the limits within which their nature is good, and they become wicked.

———

The marriage of the soul and the body. . . . Their agreement is delicious, but their disputes are cruel.

———

To warm himself in the sun of laziness . . .

———

Passions are only natural. It is the lack of repentance that corrupts.

———

The evening meal is the joy of the day.

———

How it happens that only in looking for words do we find
thoughts.

———

We have philosophized badly.

———

To hear with the eyes, to see with the ears, to represent with
air, to circumscribe in a small space great voids and full-
nesses. What am I saying? Immensity itself and all matter,
such are the incontestable and easily verified marvels that
are perpetually at work in speaking and writing.

———

Hollowed ideas. The beautiful meaning we find in this
word when we consider its good part. Hollowed like a palace and not like a cave. Hollowed; you can enter and find
marvels there, riches and beauty, greatness and pleasure.
Hollowed and transparent like crystal vases made of celestial essences. Hollowed like the cedar columns in which
treasures are hidden.

———

But the voice is not made only of air, but of air modeled by
us, impregnated by our heat and enveloped like some kind
of skin by the vapor of our inner atmosphere accompanied
by some emanation that gives it a certain shape and certain
properties capable of producing effects upon other minds.

———

Heaven will abolish the language in which these works are written.

———

To foresee with power is to see. What one foresees in this way makes present.

———

The earth is a point in space, and space is a point in the mind. By mind I understand here the spiritual element, the world's fifth element, the space of everything, the bond of all things, for all things are there, live there, move there, die there, are born there.—Mind . . . the last hold of the world.

———

There are those to whom one must advise madness.

———

Souls must not be taken to the brothel.—And: it is perfectly acceptable to go to a brothel, but no one must be taken there.
    Nota. Repentance.

———

When you want transparency, the finite, the smooth and the beautiful, you must polish for a long time.

———

Children. Let the child earn his name.

———

Our mind must not be more difficult than our taste, nor our judgment more severe than our conscience.

———

What is so finished, so exact in its expression and, in a word, so perfect, has a kind of form so determined and solid that the imagination of the reader has nothing to do and nothing to react to and therefore does not open its memory to appropriate it and retain it. We leave this memory before ourselves, to admire it, but outside of us. We are struck and not penetrated. There is nothing fluid or pithy about it, except perhaps that the thought in itself is so ethereal that it dematerializes the word.

———

Minds. Exist almost alone. Matter is used only to give them an envelope. It is a simple effigy: its weight and intensity are only an appearance. And nevertheless we speak of mass, of thickness, and of enormous weights. It is because we ourselves are inexpressibly light of matter. A speck of dust in the eye seems as hard as a pebble. It is because our eye is tender. A piece of straw against the pupil is as strong as a beam of wood. A hand in front of our view blocks it like a mountain. It is because the visual orbit is a point of extreme delicacy.

———

To know how many millions of leagues the earth is from the sun. It is a decidedly useless number to know, for it serves absolutely nothing. But to know how to measure this distance and how it has been measured is not useless. The fact is nothing, but the discovery of it is beautiful. I mean that the industry that led to it is worthy of admiration and can be usefully applied to more important measurements.

———

Clocks must regulate watches, just as laws must regulate particular actions. But the sun must regulate the clocks and justice must regulate the laws.

———

Adventurous minds, which wait for and receive their ideas only from chance.

————

Ink and paper should not be used in the way the air and the voice are used. We must not be forced to listen too long to those who cannot escape us. Some are much more interested in explaining their thought than in making it heard. It is enough, however, to make it heard. Instead of speaking, they compose. This is bad writing. There are, however, occasions when an air of concern, of attention, and even affectation can be suitable. . . .

————

We use for passions the stuff that has been given to us for happiness.

————

Of the necessity of reforming ideas in order to reform judgments.

————

My soul lives in a place where the passions have passed by and where I have known them all.

————

Lions, bulls; images of strength are everywhere, whereas images of wisdom are nowhere.

————

He gives his body up to pleasure, but not his soul.

————

Art is another nature that men have made. I call it nature because it has always been present; wherever there are men, they paint, they sing, they build.

———

We must treat our lives as we treat our writings, put them in accord, give harmony to the middle, the end, and the beginning. In order to do this we must make many erasures.

———

Strong and concise style. This must be the end, not the beginning. Refine what is subtle, change the solid into fluid, and the fluid into smoke: stop with the vapor, the cloud, etc.

———

Children and people with weak minds ask if the story is true. People with healthy minds want to know if it is moral, if it is naive, if it must be believed.

———

Dreams of love. Those of ambition. The dreams of piety.

———

When the image masks the object, when one makes a body out of shadow, when the word debauches the mind in charming it, when the expression pleases so much that we no longer go beyond it to penetrate the meaning, when the figure itself absorbs all our attention, we are stopped on the path. The road has been taken for the dwelling place. A bad guide is leading us.

———

Let us remember that everything is double.

———

We must not entrust children with fire, nor the furious with
iron.

———

Arrival of Bonaparte.

———

They are capable? Yes, but they are not respected.

———

. . . like regret, which is the salt of absence and image . . .

———

But in fact what is my art? What is the name that distinguishes this art from others? What end does it propose?
What does it produce? What does it give birth to and make
exist? What do I pretend to do and what do I want to do in
doing it?
        Is it writing in general, to assure myself of being read?
The one ambition of so many people! Is that all I want? Am I
no more than a polymath? Or do I have a class of ideas that is
easy to label and whose nature, character, merit, and use can
be determined?
        This must be examined attentively, at great length, un-
til I know the answer.

———

Children are well cared for only by their mothers and men
only by their wives.

———

——Of destructive power . . .

———

Few men, in these great political dramas, are capable of inventing a role, many are capable of playing it.

——

Old men, when neglected, have no more wisdom.

——

Plato is the Rabelais of abstractions.

——

Don't throw your mind into flowing waters.

——

Kings no longer know how to rule.

1800

Uproot? No, but transplant.

———

How through memory a person is one, and how without it there is no more I, or at least a continuous I, no more past, no more future, nothing but a numerical and mathematical present that is susceptible neither to addition nor division.

———

The ancients extolled music because (they said) it suppressed passions (at least earthly ones). We praise it because it gives them.

———

Our eye prevents us from seeing: it is our body that prevents us from touching. Between us and the truth there are our senses, which introduce a part of the truth in us and which also separate us from it. This separation, necessary to the formation of the soul, is sensitive to it, etc.

———

There emerge from us bright shadows or images, just as there emerge dark shadows or shadows properly speaking.
     There is something luminous in the face that is not found in the other parts of the body.

———

Each man thinks not what he has been told but what he understands.

———

The word, in fact, is disembodied thought.

———

Antiquity. I prefer ruins to reconstructions.

———

That little matter was enough. That in itself it is little. From which the idea of the ancients that there was only one world.

Necessity of matter. That without it God could not have separated anything from himself and that the creation would not have taken place.

That God is being. Meaning of this word, which must be taken in its strictest sense.

———

It would be difficult to be scorned and to live virtuously. We have need of support.

———

Children. Need models more than critics.

———

God is God. Nothing is God but himself.

———

. . . the whole world.—seems no more to the eyes—than a rainbow.

The hardest matter, the matter we find the darkest, shines for them, and not only with seven colors but with a million. It is for our eyes that all the streams and interplays

of light unfold. A diamond lost in the lawn is only a stone
for the caterpillar who crawls along it, but for us it is a
source of radiant scintillations. It is a star. It is a meteor.

Thus the earth, for example . . . We are . . . Minds
are . . .

———

Of the beauty of matter.

———

All ardent people have something mad about them, and all
cold people have something stupid.

———

When I say "matter is appearance," I do not pretend to chal-
lenge its reality, but, on the contrary, to give a true idea of its
real precariousness.

———

Every stone is a paste that has dried. Every metal is a body in
fusion that has cooled and hardened. All matter is tensile, or
fusible, or malleable, or all can be divided into invisible and
impalpable parts by crushing and pulverization, if the body
is solid, and by evaporation if it is already fluid. Marble, lead,
can become a cloud, from evaporation to evaporation.

Wood is composed of lines or cores pressed against each
other; it is fusible. Stone is made of coagulated dust grains; it
is fusible; crystal is a hardened water. Pumice stone is
charred: it is the white coal of a stone; it has little water.
Water, as the poets say, is a liquid crystal.

———

Every surface offers a network in which transverse lines
cross in every direction. . . .

A leaf of water, a thinned leaf. . . . A window is a hardened leaf, a leaf of glass. It is a sort of vaporous efflores-
cence. . . .
     Enamel, color . . .

——

Analysis: in morality, in cooking.

——

What is closest to our senses and farthest from our soul.

——

Descartes's noises. His physics has too much commotion.
Newton's offers us a more silent world, but too naked, too
lifeless.

——

Of all bodies, fire is the most susceptible to receiving light;
but is it luminous in itself?

——

Numbers exist,—for they exist in our mind,—and it exists.

——

A knowledge that corks the mind.

——

Only one grain of matter was needed to create the world.
But a whole world was needed to create one soul. It is a
work that cannot be done with little.
     First, an envelope of celestial matter is needed so that it
can be shaped. This envelope must be placed in a thousand
others and these thousand others in a body. This body must
then be surrounded by air, this air then filled with effluvium
by means of water, then, if it is too full, emptied by means

of fire, and man then given a pedestal. There must be the earth, there must be the sea, there must be the stars, there must be the world. I have said: "The world is a place."

———

The more I demean matter to make man stand out, the more I call attention to it and give it dignity.

———

Descartes must be reproached for his machines but not his ghosts. Too much and not too little materiality ruined his physics and his subtle matter is not subtle enough. He offers filings and dust to the imagination rather than air and ether.

———

We can see in the example provided by Saunderson that in this century one can know optics perfectly without having the slightest idea about vision.

———

He who has the abstract idea of a thing understands it; but only he who can make it understood is able to make it imaginable. Yes.

———

Neither pain nor pleasure exists outside our soul, and nevertheless these are realities more important and more real than iron, lead, marble, and all bodies taken together.

———

Of the world known by the ancients.—That it seemed more in keeping with the range of human intelligence. That this is because they knew better than we do how to envisage all things in a manner appropriate to placing them in their minds. That our minds are still astonished by our new dis-

coveries and that instead of detaching ourselves from this
affectation we affect a type of eloquence that continually
strengthens it within us. That instead of enlarging our
thoughts we enlarge the objects of our thoughts, presenting
ourselves with the extraordinary and seeking to astonish
our eyes. That instead of raising our minds above the world
and all things we raise all things above our minds. That we
turn ourselves into dwarfs in order to produce giants and diminish ourselves to make our conceptions more colossal.
That the mind must dominate everything and that when it
is dominated this means it is in the wrong place.

——

My vapors stop at my stomach.

——

Truth consists of having the same idea about something
that God has.

——

Not only are there innate ideas, but *immediate truths*, which
we feel, without intervention, without any intermediary.

——

Everything is a game except what makes the soul better or
worse.

——

There are truths that instruct, perhaps, but they do not illuminate. In this class are all the truths of reasoning.

——

The old age of men resembles their childhood. Without ex-
ception.

——

To breathe pleasure . . .

———

The least thing put between God and us separates us from him. Let us overcome it to be one with him.

    Between him and us there must be a veil, but not a wall.

———

The nightingale . . .

———

Lively minds and passionate men whose hearts, one might say, beat too fast.—The effect of a pendulum that swings too fast.

———

Echo: *vocis imago.*

———

In water, in our eyes, in our mirrors. We say that an object "paints itself there." To follow this idea. That vision is made through colors.

    Our eyes, water, and mirrors are canvasses for portraits in which objects are represented faithfully through the colors they send out; and not only are the features of objects represented there, but also their mobility in action.

    That in the arts, not just painting, but also simple drawing, things exist through colors, as well as in writing. Nothing can be separated and made distinct in our eyes except through two or more colors.

———

A body paints itself in giving off its colors.

———

Life enters there, in the same way a lighted candle placed in a lantern also carries light.

———

We are worth more when someone looks at us. And, because of this, an eye is always watching us.

———

Let us remember this.—What?—That it is not the sun in the sky that we see, but the sun at the back of our retina.

———

On Berkeley. To say there are figures without bodies is to pretend there are embroideries without material.

———

Light. I cannot be satisfied with little.
    Shyness and erasures. It is impossible for me to say something foolish without being aware of it.
    And then it is not the word that concerns me, it is the thought, which is still not entirely mine, and which I look for uselessly in the sentence. In general, my spirit of good faith rarely runs after words, except to find its thought.

———

The world and the room; books and the magic lantern.

———

Solitude gives an *I*.
    I that gives solitude. It is in our thoughts, and the one the world gives is in our feelings. Because solitude grows accustomed to seeing, to contemplating; and the world, to acting for itself.

———

You have searched in vain, you have found nothing but envelopes. Open a hundred, open a thousand, you will always be stopped before opening the last. You think you have touched the essence when you take off the outer skins. You take the homunculus for the animal. But it is much deeper. These worms, these needles, etc., are only . . . The true principle of life, the seed, the essence, the point that holds the animal, etc.

In each drop is a drop, in each point another point.

—The last is a worm; but what is inside the worm?

Nota. In opposition, works of art that have nothing inside them.

———

Politeness is the art of being bored without boredom or (if you prefer) of bearing boredom without being bored.

———

Pride swells the brain. Vanity carries with it smoke, minds. Hatred tightens the heart. Love warms the lungs. Admiration stops the heart. We breathe through desire. We want to pump up all that delights, that dilates. Sadness is inaction.

The love that comes from the blood, the love that comes from the soul.

———

Sneezes of the mind. The palace of sneezes.

———

Bonaparte in Milan. His speech to the patriots.

———

Music.—Singing demands another use of the throat and has a different voice character from that of speaking.

Singing is not just fitting words and noises together
with a certain exactitude and precision. Singing presents
our ears with a voice and accents that move the imagination.
Those who sing well have an echo in their throat and an
unidentifiable softness. Those who sing in the way they
speak do not sing, but they speak in cadence. Song must be
to speech what verse is to prose.

———

Nothing that is proved is obvious; for what is obvious
shows itself and cannot be proved.

———

God's memory. His imagination.

———

"The sound must seem an echo to the sense." This expression is from Pope. It is very beautiful.

———

The mind of every author has its faults. But every author
does not show his faults in his works. We pardon those who
know how to hide them.

———

To speak with his imagination, but to think with his reason.

———

To make oneself ignorant.

———

I would like thoughts to follow one another in a book like
stars in the sky, with order, with harmony, but effortlessly
and at intervals, without touching, without mingling; and
nevertheless not without finding their place, harmonizing,

arranging themselves. Yes, I would like them to move without interfering with one another, in such a way that each could survive independently. No overstrict cohesion; but no incoherence either; the lightest is monstrous.

———

Let us not confuse what is merely intelligible, that is to say, easily understood, with what is clear.

———

To make enough space to open his wings.

———

The poet must not cross an interval with a step when he can cross it with a leap.

———

Rubens. Concave eye, microscope.

———

To play with sounds (or words) when the results of this game do not lead to any confusion of meaning, but on the contrary lead to clarity—this game gives pleasure.

———

Thus, names are correctly applied only when they are *necessary names*, and they are *necessary names* only when no others can signify what they signify,—and, if they do not already exist, they would have to be invented.

———

Notions that seem to impregnate the mind.

———

Resemblances. And whether they do not sometimes work through a sort of reflection, which the animated body is capable of imbibing, so to speak, and persistently.—Farmers' wives and their chickens.

———

The things that we know when not thinking of them.

———

Where do ideas go?—They go into the memory of God.
    Nota. To define light to a blind man, noise to a deaf man, thought to an idiot.

———

Young people . . . They give their minds much exercise but little food.

———

Repentance consumes.—And what does it consume?—It consumes the faults and the tendency that caused them.

———

Ideas never lack for words. It is words that lack ideas. As soon as the idea has come to its last degree of perfection, the word blossoms; or, if you like, it blossoms from the word that presents it and clothes it.

———

Blind people are cheerful because their minds are not distracted by the representation of things that can please them and because they have even more ideas about spectacles than we do.

———

If a blind man asked me: "What is light?" I would answer: "What makes us see."—"What is seeing?"—"It is to have an idea of what is before our eyes without having to think about it."

——

Those mental traits that lead us to hideous obscurities.

——

Thoughts that cannot survive the test of the open air and that evaporate as soon as we take them out of our room. To put them to the test of isolation. Take them out of the book where you found them: they do not endure.

——

The air is sonorous, and sound is made of air, of air that is uttered, vibrant, shaped, articulated.

——

But the idea of the nest in the bird's mind, where does it come from?

——

An idea can be produced from something or from nothing, and provided this nothing is constant, the idea has no less existence or importance.

——

That we cannot conceive of the idea of time without the idea of eternity, nor the idea of place without that of space and infinite extension.

——

When? you say. I answer you:—When I have circumscribed my sphere.

——

Animate flour. Leavening, in effect, is animation, life, a mind, a soul put into the dough.

It is through the imagination that one is a metaphysician.

——

On the need for the beautiful,—natural to certain minds and highly developed in others. Defects of style of which it is the cause.

This need for the beautiful creates a habit, almost a necessity, of putting into the expression much art and force when the thought or the subject in themselves have no great merit. With this character and type of mind one cannot write simply or naturally except when one has thoughts that are beautiful. Wait for them.

——

Of words that take up so much attention that they turn us away from the thought. (Vid. supra.) These shocking, astonishing, striking words are sometimes the only way to make a thought palpable. It can be articulated only through them. They are especially capable (and they alone), they alone are capable of bringing out the attitudes and movements of the mind, operations that are just as agreeable, just as useful, and just as important to know as the thoughts themselves.

——

To know: it is to see inside oneself.

——

Perhaps (and probably) it would be true to say that we cannot conceive of anything except what we can see in our minds.

———

Truth. To surround it with figures and colors, so that it can been seen.

———

It is very difficult to be wise (through the mind); it is not difficult to be wise occasionally and by chance, but it is difficult to be wise assiduously and by choice.

———

Everyone makes and has need of making a world other than the one he sees.

———

Leibnitz and Spinoza.—The realm of abstraction. The first offers its perfection, the second nothing but its flaws.

———

Condillac. Perception (he says) produces attention. But attention leads to perception. We can therefore consider it as preexistent to perception and in fact it often is. But one would answer that the first perception came before the first act of attention. That matters little, and it will always be true to say that in the formed man who is able to . . . otherwise.

———

To analyze, to deconstruct.—What they so emphatically call analysis is what we would call division when speaking simply.

The subject must be analyzed in terms of itself, that is, it must be considered from all sides and examined part by part, turned and turned again. Everything must be said concisely and simultaneously after having been examined repeatedly and at length. The writer must be like a painter. The painter considers his model trait by trait, but it is the whole that he shows. It is not ray by ray, but through facets, that the light shines for us.

———

Phantoms of thoughts! . . .

———

If prayer does not change our destiny, it changes our feelings—which is no less useful.

———

How admiration contributes to the peace of the human mind and is necessary to it.

———

Every house: temple, empire, school.

———

In our writings thought seems to move like a man who is walking straight ahead. On the other hand, in the writings of the ancients, thought seems to move like a bird that glides and advances by turning round and round.

———

Everything seems naked to eyes that have never seen without veils. Nothing can please them for very long.

1801

History, like perspective, has need of distance.

——

Close your eyes and you will see.

——

This man too has need of perspective. You come too close to him with your eye.

——

Vision is made by the joining of two lights.—Add. March 19: And if objects shine toward us, we shine toward objects.

——

Minds that are made of material, and so much so they spread only shadow, like bodies that are opaque.

——

To want to know invariably and fixedly what is only vague, and vaguely what is fixed and solid, is finally to know neither one nor the other.

——

And what am I but an atom in a ray?

——

The poet. He paints passions under glass.

———

Christianity. We cannot speak against it without anger, nor speak for it without love.

———

Logic is a demi-geometry and metaphysics is a demi-poetry that gives a transparent body to what has no body, just as poetry gives a soul.

———

Another feature of pure and elementary truth: pleasure; the pleasure the soul receives from it.

———

Figure, movement. Everything happens, says Pascal, from figure and movement. To say in this case that everything happens from movement, for every figure is no more than the lingering trace of a movement that has already ceased. Thus the letters I am forming now, for example, are only the pen's lingering trace of the movement of my hand.

———

Objects must be described only in order to describe the feelings they evoke in us.

———

There grows up between our senses and all our perceptions, between the shocks of all things and all their commotions, between all agitations and our resolve, a distance, an interval, a time, a void, a space where everything becomes calm, tempered, dim, silent, slow.

———

I have not seen you since, but you have often appeared to me in my dreams.

——

In those days they took allusions from the world and today we are forced to take them from books. This is a disadvantage.

——

Yes, we have three eyes, we also have three ears (as the Chinese author said). For in addition to the two eyes and two ears of the body, we must also consider the ear of the soul, the invisible eye of the mind.

The imagination is an eye where images remain forever.

——

At ten o'clock this evening. My poor mother! My poor mother!

——

"To bury your life" is lovely. (Volt. Irèn.)

——

It is the bell that moves, but you who ring. It is the sun that shines, but you who see. The nourishment is in the meat, but the taste is in you. Fire gives or creates warmth, but it is you who feel it.

Harmony is in the one who listens: yes, as effect; but not as cause.

——

I like Leibnitz's expression *the soul carries the body*. And observe that everywhere and in everything, what is subtle car-

ries what is compact; and what is light holds in suspension
all that is heavy. Admit it, at least in the sense of——and as
the most beautiful conception of the human mind.

———

This stone in my hand, it demands glory.

———

Somber and unhappy lovers of a murderous equality.

———

I thus call space everything that is not myself, that is not determined.

———

In the places where I live. I always want much sky to be
mixed with little earth; this can only be done when . . .

———

And what do the diverse pleasures roused in us by books,
paintings, conversations, etc., consist of, if not that they
show us (more or less) the nakedness of thoughts, ideas,
minds, souls more or less whole, perfect, complete? And
what pleases you in the fortuitous arrangements or order-
ings of raw nature, if not that they more or less resemble a
thought, a drawing, drawings or thoughts that please us,
and all the more so because they are not rigorously determined, which gives us the advantage of conceiving of them
in the way we like best?

———

A thought is a thing as real as a cannon ball.

———

One must write with effort in centuries of bad taste.—
Why?—Facility would reinforce the reader's weariness.
How?

———

To seek the truth. But, as you are seeking and as you are
waiting, what will you do, what will you think, what will
you practice, what rules must you follow?

———

The spectacle has changed, but our eyes are the same.

———

No, I am not angry with myself, but I am angry with
books.

———

This young man you call Bonaparte . . .

———

Everything beautiful is indeterminate.

———

To use reason to give us passions.—Monstrosities.—No
. . .—How.

———

It is an opera without orchestra, a song without accompaniment. It demands an airy style that does not touch the
ground.

———

Do not choose for your wife any woman you would not
choose as your friend if she were a man.

———

Accountable for their deeds—But, for me—it is my thoughts I account for.

——

Religion adheres powerfully to the dead.

——

Beautiful works. Genius begins them, but labor alone finishes them.

——

Of the unfortunate need to please oneself.

——

Newton. How ripe his apple was.

——

Banish from words everything equivocal, everything indeterminate; make them, as they say, into invariable numbers: if there is no more play in the word, from then on there is no more eloquence or poetry; all that is mobile and variable in the soul's affections would remain without possible expression. But what did I say, banish . . . I say more. If you banished all abuse from words, there would not even be any axioms. (Vid. d'Alembert, Discourse on the Encyclopedia.) It is the equivocality, the uncertainty, that is to say, the suppleness of words that is one of their great advantages for creating an exact usage.

——

Faculty of inventing languages—is an industry natural to our intelligence.

——

In the end, God loves each man as much as he loves mankind. Weight and number are as nothing in his eyes. Eternal, immense, infinite, he has only immense loves.

———

Expiate dreams.

———

How it is always through the beyond and not through the within that all languages become corrupted. Through the beyond of their usual sound, their natural energy, their habitual force, etc. It is fracas that accompanies their decadence and luxury that corrupts them.

———

We are all old children, more or less serious, more or less filled with ourselves.

———

We still know how to mark the hours, but no longer how to ring them. The carillon of our clocks is missing.

———

It seems more difficult to me to be a modern than to be an ancient.

1802

Floods of passions. It would nevertheless be better to raise
the dikes for them.

——

That God has the idea of our ideas. Now, if God has the idea
of our ideas, it follows that, etc.

A presumption in favor of the resemblance of our ideas
with the object. Our identity with God? But who would
dare to speak in this way? Let us simply say therefore: our
participation in the divine intelligence.

——

From this day forward, to give up Locke, and to agree never
to read another word he has written.

——

What will you think of pleasures when you no longer enjoy
them?

——

The only thing Newton invented was the how much.

——

The things we believe are difficult to conceive of because it
is difficult to talk about them.

——

In fact everything (according to Descartes) everything happens through figure and movement. That is the fixed point from which his mind proceeded to all its operations, the result of his explanations. That is his doctrine, summed up in a few words. Goodbye, Descartes!

The white markings of the snow, here and there, scattered on the greenness in time of thaw.

The shadow of smoke, in the sunlight.—Jan. 21: in the ice.

All beings come from little, and little is needed for them to come to nothing.

You say that books are soon read, but they are not soon understood. To digest them, etc. To understand a beautiful or great thought perhaps requires the same amount of time it takes to have it, to conceive of it. To penetrate a thought and to produce a thought are almost the same action.

Piety is a cure.

Dream. Lost memory.

We can say of all poems that are not born as if from themselves and delivered (if we can speak this way) from the heart and womb of revery: these are poems that do not have a mother—*prolem sine matre cretam*. They all have something imperfect about them, something unfinished.

———

Lafontaine. The expression in his verse is imperfect, undecided. But the poet's disposition is very marked and the work pleases because of that. This shows that the highly pronounced attitude of a man who dreams is pleasant to us, even if we don't know what he is dreaming about.

———

When I glow . . . I lose my oil.

———

In our efforts to remember, we are searching.—Where are we searching? Where? In our idea,—in the canvas, in the mirror, in the atmosphere that is between our senses and our mind.

———

We are in life more to act than to know. But to realize even this, that we are in life, etc., we must know. And even this is a kind of acting, knowing. It is one of our duties.

———

One would say that in such dark eyes there is a flame without light.

———

Imagined harmonies. If they are not a physical fact, they are at least a human fact, and because of that, a reality.

———

If a superior intelligence wanted to give an account of human things to the inhabitants of heaven and to give an exact idea of them, he would express himself like Homer.

———

I pass my life chasing after butterflies—considering the ideas that conform to generally held ideas as good, and the others simply as mine.

———

. . . and the minds that are sympathetic to my own.

———

Balance. We look for it in order to go to sleep. If interior, easy to find. If not, difficult.—So little needed to establish it: the folding or unfolding of a sheet is enough.

———

Scrupulous taste. Scrupulous people rarely do great things.

———

That is true, a king without religion always seems a tyrant.

———

The revolution chased my mind from the real world by making the world too horrible for me.

———

Those ideas that dispose the mind to produce the truth.

———

In morality (a science of practice and circumstances) the individual is made for society. But in metaphysics (and even

in religion), a science of real essences, society is made for individuals.

———

It is even easier to be wrong about truth than about beauty.

———

In order for a style to be considered good, it must, so to
speak, detach itself from the paper, in the same way that the
colors and figures detach themselves from a good painting.

———

Men do not want to learn unfashionable truths except when
they are spared the pains of attention.

———

It seems that Plato has too much and that there is too little in
Aristotle. From which, in the first, an abundance carried to
superfluity, and in the other a precision or brevity that leads
to obscurity.

———

Speak more softly to be better heard by a deaf public.

———

To call everything by its name.

———

Illusas que auro vestes (Virg.) Magic is needed everywhere. It
exists in painting through color, in sculpture through
[   ] and in music through tone, which creates the
effect of speaking without words. Even a beautiful fabric
has magic: silk, a fine sheet, velvet, and even what they call
"fine whites."

Illusion based on reality, that is the secret of the fine arts—in fact, of all art.

———

We speak to ourselves in metaphors. We are naturally led to it as a method of better understanding ourselves and of retaining our thoughts more easily—which we then label in a kind of container.

"In a container of light." Y.

———

Metaphysics. A vast science in which everything is true, even what is contradictory, as in a vast countryside the same towers are both round and square.

———

There are only two kinds of beautiful writing, that which has a great fullness of sound, meaning, soul, warmth, and life, and that which has a great transparency.

———

We have it in our soul, but we hardly ever put into our life what we put into our writings.

———

If I weigh myself down, everything is lost.

———

In every piece of music, not everything is music, and in every poem not everything is poetry.

———

Fear feeds the imagination.

———

Happy people strike me as children; people who are too serious and especially those who are proud strike me as
dwarfs. Or rather, those who are vain strike me as children;
those who are prideful strike me as dwarfs.—Children and
dwarfs. Their difference: a dwarf is the size of a child, but
with a man's face.

———

The first act of a man who finds God displeasing is to say to
himself: I must arrange the world without him.

———

Imagining is good, provided you do not believe you see
what can only be imagined.

———

Lost spirit. Judges without justice, priests without religion.

———

Sensibility that comes from the nerves. Opinions have a
great influence on it and can lead to cruelty. Examples in the
revolution.

———

(At the baths.) Piety defends us from ourselves; modesty
defends us from others.

———

(5 in the morning. Insomnia.) Everything must have its sky.
To be put everywhere.

———

There are many situations in life that we suddenly feel we
have seen in dreams.

———

The sky or perspective is what makes poetry. The echo is what makes music. The bright and the dark in painting. The dreamed, or the hollow of the brain, in all things. The soul, finally, or the mind and the spiritual world, etc. Space.

——

Tragic actors. Express sensation more than sentiment.

——

Fixed style.—Of a man who has dreamed a great deal with himself, or of a man who has arranged in advance the style he will write in. Between these two *fixed styles* there is a great difference. The second is mere labor, a mechanism of professional work. The other is a true operation of the mind. And it is natural; reflection is as natural as flowing water.

——

All beautiful words are susceptible to more than one meaning (or signification).

——

Every excess is a mistake.

——

The phrase: "One dies because one has lived."

——

Two things can never be the object of the same thought at the same time unless there is some symmetry *uniting* them or turning the two things into a single thing.
Symmetry. Or correspondence. Secret link, etc.
Through it a middle is created (at the point of contact), a middle, I say, from which one can perceive the extremities.

——

My memory holds no more than the essence of what I read, of what I see and even of what I think.

————

The breast. This new ornament makes those who have it and are not used to it blush.

————

Those minds in which there is always something beyond their thought and, so to speak, that do not have limits.

————

To truth by way of illusion.

————

Sad science that teaches blind men to speak of light and colors and that persuades them they can even make judgments about these things.

————

A heart of beef is not a heart. (Mme J.)

————

The child speaks words with his memory long before he speaks them with his tongue.

————

1803

Nothing is more difficult for children than reflection. That is because the last and essential destination of the soul is seeing, is knowing, and not reflecting. Reflection is one of the labors of life, a means of getting somewhere, a path, a passage, and not a center. Everything always tends towards its final destination. To know and be known, these are the two points of rest. This will be the happiness of souls.

——

The weather strikes me on the head. I feel it rattle my teeth.

——

. . . but in the end a year comes when you find that you are getting old.

——

To treat these materials well (metaphysical subjects), we must get as far away from the philosophers and as close to the poets as we can.

——

Stacking the dead on top of each other.

——

Those heavy minds that annoy us with their weight and immobility. You can't make them fly or swim. Because they

87

don't know how to help themselves, they grab hold of you
and drag you down.

——

Minds that love to wheel around like birds, to rise up, to
glide, to wander, to cleave the air in order to come back to a
fixed point, a solid and precise point.

——

To know how to walk in the night, to have a goal, to reach it
in the darkness, the shadows.

——

That the history of our thoughts (in spite of us and without
our knowledge) is found in our language. This notion of
G.'s is very good, very right, and the idea is very true.—
Observation: G. never said this. I was wrong. He simply
said that language in general should be considered a monu-
ment to human reason.

——

Everything is made through images. They enter us through
all the other senses, as through the eye. An echo (they say) is
an image of the voice. All our affections are produced by
images of touching. Our whole body is a mirror.

——

Pleasures that we can perceive only when they no longer
give us pleasure.

——

Someone said of an asthmatic who was being very sweet
and patient in his suffering: "One would like to breathe for
him."

——

The natural pace of the mind. And how it should move so as not to get worn out by quickness or bogged down and made impatient by slowness.

———

Disagreeable shortcuts of style.

———

Fleeting irrelevancies often serve to stamp solid objects in our memory; a sound, a song, an accent, a voice, a smell engrave forever in our mind the memory of certain places, because these small things were what made up our pleasure or boredom there.

———

Yes. Whether thought can exist outside the mind in the same way a word can exist outside the mouth.

———

Turning round in my mind for a long time.
 Not to write, at such moments, with one's resources.
 To gather my earth. First of all, it must be left to stand. Later, there will be nothing left to do but grind it up.
 To make work easier.

———

The same feature that is agreeable when it is fleeting becomes hideous when it remains fixed. That is because mobility is the essence of what is agreeable.

———

Everything must be precise in it and yet nothing should be too tight.

———

Let the work be complete and round.

——

In fact the word is the sign of a thought and writing is the sign of the word. That is to say, it is only the sign of another sign.

——

. . . because, what must be put in the work and what must be left out is infinite.

——

For the first form and idea of a work must be a space, a simple place where the material can be put, arranged, not a material to be put somewhere and arranged.

——

Debts shorten life.

——

Minds incapable of care. And: thoughts that have stayed in the mind for a long time. "I lived with the rose." And that: the same taste that leads us to do something well forces us to redo it, to do little, to do slowly, making it difficult for us to approve of what we have done. And that: the best is the enemy of the good only when we look for it and not when we see it. Even more, we do not do well except when we know where the best is and when we are assured that we have touched it and hold its power within us. And that: it is not things that please, but the impression the mind makes on itself, that it puts into itself and leaves there, for only the mind pleases the mind, only the soul pleases the soul. Except one single thing, whose power the mind takes little part in and is independent of thought and will, being necessary to the multiplication of souls and the survival of the human race.

———

The thoughts that come to us are worth more than the ones we seek.

———

To know what one must forbid oneself.

———

Flowers in cemeteries. They must be uprooted; this earth spoils them.—And let the skeletons smile. Horrible amusements.

———

Chateaubriand. We inhabit the same regions but we do not bring back the same curiosities.

———

Collections, thoughts. The man shows himself in them, if the author does not.

———

I have many forms for ideas, but not enough forms for phrases.

———

My lynx eyes.

———

I feel the almond in the shell, the water in the earth, the fire in the stone.

———

To have an attention so firm that it sees ideas as if they were
things, and in the same way eyes see the realities before
them, in the same way they are painted on the retina.

———

What we write with difficulty is written with more care, en-
graves itself more deeply.

———

. . . this poetry of thought.

———

. . . . and withdraw into that freedom of mind whose
charms are dangerous, according to them—but when
treated correctly it is certainly the most useful thing in the
world.

———

All nightingales do not sing equally well, nor do all roses
smell the same.

———

Music has seven letters, writing has twenty-six notes.

———

Rigorously to avoid encountering the limits of your mind.

———

Widowhood rejuvenates them.

———

Words like so many tiny wheels.

———

Lightning flashes that cross the mind and illuminate so
quickly they are hardly noticed. In such cases, more is seen

than retained. Thus, whoever does not observe himself carries within him some experience he does not know about.

———

In us there is a corner where we are always young and almost children. This is not because our thoughts lack meaning or gravity, but because we are not destined in life for any serious role.

———

To live with oneself, that is to say . . .
   "To live medicinally" is not always to live unhappily, no matter what the proverb says, if during this time one lives with oneself.
   Not how long he has lived, but how long he has lived with himself and in himself.
   In oneself is to have no movements other than those that come from us or from our consent. And with onself is to feel nothing that is not known to us. It is to be the witness, the confidant, the arbitrator of all that one does and all that one says and all that one thinks. It is at once to live life and to contemplate it. It is to live known by oneself. It is to serve as one's own companion, friend, advisor. It is to age, it is . . .

———

Anger. Its fermentation is necessary to the maturing of certain soft and peaceful feelings. But if the crisis does not take place, if the fermentation leads only to its own bitterness, the operation has not borne fruit and the natural course of things has not been followed.

———

It is difficult for me to leave Paris because I must separate myself from my friends; and difficult for me to leave the country because I must separate myself from myself.

———

. . . speaking only of the head. Voice of the head, mind of the head, opinions of the head.

——

Words, and whether they are more important than sentences.

——

The silence of the pen and its advantages. Force builds up in it. Precision must flow out of it. A chatterer fallen quiet. When silence comes from force, it should make itself felt in discourse. What is hasty would be bad upon reflection.—To know how not to write—to be capable of not writing.

——

Everything has its poetry.

——

And those for whom a long old age has seemed to purify the body.

——

For an expression to be beautiful it must say more than is necessary while nevertheless saying precisely what it must. The *too much* and the *enough* must be united, there must be abundance and economy. The narrow and the wide, the little and the much, must be mingled. The sound must be brief and the meaning infinite. Example: *discentem credere opportet* (Aristot.). Everything luminous has this character. A lamp and its wick perfectly brighten not only the object for which they are used but twenty others for which one did not think of using them.

——

To write, not only with few words, but with few thoughts.

——

It would be quite possible to dance or mime one of Sterne's chapters. Even several of Montesquieu's chapters. The chapter on despotism, for example.

——

The voice is an aid to intelligence.

——

The soul. It can raise up the body.

——

Luckily, I never feel at one time more than half my pains.

——

Two sorts of truths: I. what must be thought, II. what must be done.

——

They speak to the ear, I want to speak to the memory.

——

Yes, a flame without smoke, a light without vapors, that is what I want, but that is what is impossible to have often and even less so always.

——

Of certain beauties, certain thoughts, certain feelings, certain imaginative traits that are absolutely new. No one was expecting them. Their novelty makes people indecisive. We are afraid to hazard our judgment, to compromise the honor of our opinion. We decide to approve of these things late. We dare not taste them; we want proofs to be provided first. We are completely surprised that these things continue to charm us long after we have seen them for the first time.

———

Natural! natural! yes, no doubt, natural; but what do they mean by this word? Are the sounds of a flute natural, if by this word we understand a thing that only nature makes?

———

Finally, when you can't find the word you were looking for, you put down the word that was there, which might lead you to it without your knowing how. This is in fact natural, for nature carries you to it.

———

Yes, you; because you write with ink. But I write with colors.

———

And everything comes from the entrails, everything, even the least expression. This is perhaps inconvenient, but necessary: I submit to it.

———

Attention is sustained (in poetry) by the amusement of the ear. Prose does not have this advantage. Might it have? I try. But I think not.

———

As the sea touches the moon through its vapors, and the sun, through the length of its rays, touches the earth—distances.

1804

Then there comes into languages a facility and an over-abundance that, if you want to become a great writer, you must oppose with difficulties, with a sure taste, a meditated choice. When you find a torrent, obstacles must be placed in it.

———

Strength in organization and weakness in carrying out the material. Like an automaton whose elasticity would be exquisite if the wood were not too thin or too fragile.
    There I am: a flattering self-portrait.

———

To survive one's passions and not one's strengths. Happy.

———

A poetic vapor, a cloud, that is resolved in prose.

———

This wisdom. It is constant, but mobile.

———

Those useless phrases that come into the head. The mind is grinding its colors.

———

Severe taste and prodigious imagination.

———

It is beautiful enough to be seen, but not to be dreamed.

———

God. There are many things that should be left in life and not put into books.

———

The germinating grass that stirs the earth and leaves around its root the traces of this movement. See the fields.

———

Memory and rhythm.

———

It is a key; what difference if it is gold or iron? It can open things.

———

I have to grind my sentences; and that is the most difficult thing.

———

Not only the grinding of sentences, but grouping them; and to detach masses from one another: another difficult operation.

———

And note how in each true meditation a moment of rest follows each movement.

———

The drop of dew and the diamond: colors and dew play in
one and in the other.
      —Like those dark clouds I saw embroidered with light.

———

When the author speaks to himself instead of speaking to
the reader.

———

Everything that is exact is short.

———

I am not at the end.

———

"But he doesn't finish his sentences," (he said). And they
don't finish their thoughts.—To finish their thoughts.—To
finish one's thought! It is a long process, it is rare. It gives intense pleasure. Because every finished thought easily enters
the mind. They don't have the same need to be beautiful in
order to please. It is enough for them to be finished. The situation of the soul that has had such thoughts communicates
itself to other souls and transfers its repose to them.

———

Another rain and another clear sky than the rain and clear
sky of other men.

———

The body. Like a piece of clothing that wears out.

———

These thoughts form not only the foundation of my work,
but of my life.

———

To paint and adorn ideas. Advantages, inconveniences.

——

Fever. In the swamps of reason.

——

It is not mental repose they seek, but mental laziness.

——

Enter oneself (we say). When one enters oneself, one sees God.

——

God. All other beings are distinguished by their shadow, but he is distinguished by his light.

——

Lumine vestit. We are all and always clothed with God and invested with his light. We can however not think about it, in the same way we can not think about ourselves.

——

The finger and the eye of the worker continually placed on his work.

——

Descartes. His imaginary world is not an imaginable world. In it the mind finds matter everywhere, and figures rather than form. (For the form is the figure of the figure, the figure is the body of the form, the form is the exterior soul of a body.) Descartes has thus made the imagination do what it does not like to do. He has made it arrange stones. It wants to be an architect: he has restricted it to being a mason.

——

Infinity! We have the sight of it more than the idea.

————

The heart must walk ahead of the mind, and indulgence ahead of the truth.

————

I wanted to bypass words, I disdained them: words have had their revenge—through difficulty, etc.

————

To the question: is he guilty? must be added another question: is he incorrigible?

————

They want to shake up the world, not make it wiser.

————

"Life," (I said), "is not given to us to be known, but as a means."
　　B[onaparte] treats men this way. He does not think of knowing them and judging them, but of using them.

————

The time I once lost in pleasure I now lose in suffering.

————

When you write easily, you always think you have more talent than you really do.

————

The anecdote told today by D'Arnaud. "Where did you go, young ladies?"—"We went to see the guillotine, mama; oh dear, how horrible it was for the executioner." This grotesque displacement of pity that shows the true spirit of this century, a century in which everything has been turned upside down.

———

There is nothing serious in civil life except good and evil, vice and virtue. Everything else in it should be a game.

———

They are all false, you say? And I say: they are all true.

———

And perhaps we speak so well only when we don't know exactly what we are going to say.

———

It is not my words that I polish, but my ideas.

———

Minds that are eagles, without feathers, without wings.

———

Of those who feel God as light and of those who feel him as rules.

———

Of those who feel God as rules, as light, and of those who feel him as love.

———

Waves of light and layers of brightness.

———

In the same way crimes have increased laws, errors have increased explanations.

———

In the way a beam of light pierces a cloud, the light a fog.
Or—in the way a movement can penetrate a whole mass
without making any change in it.

———

For the subject must please, and all subjects are difficult.

———

Children are severe. Why.

———

Of those who remember their childhood and those who
only remember school.

———

Until the drop of light I need, that I am waiting for, forms
and falls.

1805

Those thoughts that come to us suddenly and that are not yet ours.

————

I know too well what I am going to say. I know it too well before writing.

————

We must try, as much as possible, not to mistrust anyone.

————

And for this reason our words have too much strength and our thoughts not enough.

This moderation which makes one robust . . .

Like those men who say cold things with warmth and weak things with strength, they have teeth and lungs, but not good reasons.

————

Thoughts that are light, clear, distinct, finished; and words that resemble their thoughts.

Words that often retain their meaning even when they are detached from the others and that please when isolated as sounds.

————

For simple light is perhaps still more beautiful than colors.

———

Glory. Lovelier to desire than to possess.

———

Opinions are things that illuminate—true meteors.

———

There are words and beauties born from the pen. But . . .

———

All things that are easy to say have already been perfectly said.

———

Once we have tasted the juice of words, the mind can no longer pass them by. We drink thought from them.

———

. . . and, since heaven willed it, to pass my life supporting the weight of my stomach.

———

Art has nothing to do with such books. They should be left to commerce.

———

——We at least could have answered him by saying that the sciences are a thing without which we could not have known that the sciences are useless.

———

And in fact when we remember a beautiful line, a beautiful word, a beautiful phrase, it is always in the air that we read

them; we see them before us, our eyes seem to read the
words in space. We do not imagine them on the paper
where they were written. On the other hand, a vulgar passage does not separate itself from the book where we read it;
and it is there that the memory sees it when it is quoted. I say
this from experience.

————

To dominate force. An iron style.

————

But if we divide what is simple, if we want to divide what
is one, if we distribute into several parts what has no joints,
we destroy it, we make it immediately unknowable. We
have axed it, destroyed it, and still we think it has been analyzed.

————

I call imagination the faculty of making palpable all that be-
longs to the mind, of incorporating what is spirit, and, in a
word, of unveiling what is invisible to itself without rob-
bing it of its nature.

————

If, during sleep, God speaks to the soul, we do not know it.

————

"The art is in hiding art." Yes, in everything that should resemble nature. But isn't there anything that should resemble art and therefore show itself?

————

My ideas! It is the house for lodging them that costs me so
much to build.

————

In the writings of J.-J. Rousseau for example, the soul is always mingled with the body and cannot be separated from it.

——

. . . passing their life in contradicting their childhood,—in erasing it.

——

To live without a body!

——

Heaven has given children a great abundance of tears.

——

Architecture of words. (Add): where everything is made with words that can hold themselves in the air. Add again: like sounds. And look for what might give sounds this quality, or what properly constitutes a sound and makes a noise what it is.

——

. . . with that laughter that seems to rejoice in evil.

——

——like those acts of justice that corrupt those who commit them.

——

All these young minds the revolution has heated up and brought to flower before their time, before their age.

——

To judge things of taste, we must give ourselves time to taste them.

——

Let us look to beautiful poetry for the material of a beautiful prose.

——

An oratorical style often has the same drawbacks as those operas in which the music prevents you from hearing the words. Here the words prevent you from seeing the thoughts.

——

All these writings of which nothing remains, like a stream (clear water rolling over small stones), but the memory of words that have fled.

——

All reflection is art.

——

This poetic nudity within words.

——

The mind. It loves to produce flowers.

——

And, in fact, when we speak, we write what we are saying in the air.

——

One can advance a long time in life without aging.

——

In simple masonry, there are no ideas; in architecture there
are. There is a conception from the soul. . . . There is
beauty wed to utility. In simple masonry, there is only utility. It houses man as a thing, as an animal, and not as an intelligence. It is concerned with the night and storms more
than with the day and peaceful weather.

But a bird's nest, a beaver's house? God had the idea for
these things and gave the animal the industry to carry out
his thought.

————

. . . and the delights of the earth. There must be
others. . . .

————

The soul speaks to itself in parables.

————

All grace (*decor*) comes from patience. And, consequently,
from some force exerted on itself.

————

Like those dreams that have pleased us. They escape us and
we vainly try to hold onto them.

————

My dreams are more amorous than my actions have ever
been.

————

Genius is the aptitude for seeing invisible things, for stirring
intangible things, for painting things that have no features.

————

The human mind. It is a subtle thing and loves subtleties.—
All causes are subtle and the effects alone are palpable.

———

In effect, if we knew perfectly what was happening in
heaven, we would be more free of it. And if we knew perfectly what existed on earth, perhaps we would no longer be
mortal.

———

Conversation.—Because they have many of those ideas that,
to be shown, have need of eyes, gestures, voice, a whole
multitude of signs that the written word does not accompany.
     One sees the soul in operation.

———

To see the world means judging the judges.

———

The more I think about it, the more I see that the mind is
something outside the soul, just as hands are outside the
body, eyes outside the head, branches outside the trunk. It
helps to *do*, but not *be* more.

———

It is not simply a matter of distinguishing between good
and evil, but also of not confusing what is laughable with
what is not. To make laughable what is not is in some way
to make bad what was good.

———

We are afraid of having and showing a small mind and we
are not afraid of having and showing a small heart.

———

One ruins the mind with too much writing.—One rusts it by not writing at all.

————

. . . like children's hair, which is always a color that will change.

————

The little cat and the piece of paper he turns into a mouse. He touches it lightly, for fear of unmasking his illusion.

————

All ways of expressing ourselves are good if they make us understood. Thus, if the clarity of our thoughts comes through better in a play of words, then the wordplay is good.

————

One must know how to enter the ideas of others and how to leave them. One must know how to leave one's own ideas and how to come back to them.

————

They say that souls have no sex; of course they do.

————

——bodies avid for a new flesh.

————

Their heads are too small for the greatness of their ideas.

————

The tulip is a flower without soul, but it seems that the rose and the lily have one. (The first is beautiful like a young girl.) The rose is a flower of flesh, the tulip is a flower of cloth, of taffeta. The lily is beautiful like a young man and we know to what beauties the rose is often compared. The tulip is a kind of wallpaper.

———

It seems that there is something spiritual in wine.

———

In every kind of debauch there enters much coldness of soul. It is a conscious and voluntary abuse of pleasure.

———

In everything mathematical there is something imperishable, because there is nothing living.

———

I resemble a poplar. This tree always seems young, even when it is old.

———

A drop of light is worth more than an ocean of darkness: is worth more, I say, be it given or received.

———

What man knows only through feeling can be explained only through enthusiasm.

———

Does God want us to love his enemies?—Yes. Why?

———

I. A better language has better opinions.—And all my stars in a sky.—All space is my canvas.
II. Stars fall to me from the mind.

———

It is above all the language for expressing these truths that has not yet been found.

———

Terrestrial by birth, celestial by origin, only our body is of this world.

———

Children are people.

———

There is no metaphysics without the ravishing of the mind, just as there is no poetry without enthusiasm.

———

A person who is never duped cannot be a friend.

1806

I don't like to write anything down on paper that I would not say to myself.

——

They cling to the gates and see only through the bars.

——

The important business of man is life, and the important business of life is death.

——

To descend into ourselves, we must first lift ourselves up.

——

Deprived for a long time of ideas that suited my mind or of a language that suited my ideas.

——

One must be an *illusionary* rather than a *visionary*.

——

Illusions come from heaven and mistakes come from us.

——

Tacitus. And all those words that are obscure only once.

——

Before using a beautiful word, make a place for it. Air is needed in front of a facade. An entablature placed in the middle of a wall indicates destruction rather than construction.

——

. . . and that I hatch my little eggs, my bird's nest; for my thoughts and my words have wings.

——

——in these times when, to express ourselves well, we must speak in a way the others do not.

——

——think nothing outside their paper.

——

I did not have good eyes nor light in my mind that day.

——

Marble is concentrated air. I would call the diamond condensed light. The world is a swollen point.

——

The little girl who hears music for the first time and cries out: "It's God speaking to us!" (In that bad novel by Mme de Genlis.)

——

Available. A thought is perfect only when it is perfectly available, that is to say when one can place it and detach it at will.

——

All those for whom style is not a game but a labor.

——

. . . burdened with the unbearable weight of ourselves.

——

Facility is the enemy of great things.

——

Metaphysics. At least the mind finds space in it. Elsewhere it finds only fullness.

——

All clear and transparent words appear to be beautiful sounds.
      Yes and *no* are not precisely clear words, but definite words. In clear words, there is more light than movement or attitude. *Yes* and *no* are what the Latins called *gestuosa verba*.

——

Of what is spiritual in matter.

——

History. We want to find moral lessons in it, but its only lessons are of politics, military art, etc.

——

What you call weakness comes from the strength of friendship.

——

Racine is the Virgil of the ignorant.

——

Beyond the brain, there is something that observes the brain itself.

——

His hope to "change color."

——

Undoubtedly, philosophy caused the Revolution. But what caused philosophy? Theological arrogance.

——

Those who never back down love themselves more than they love the truth.

——

The music and painting of the streets. Their importance.

——

Ordinary brightness is no longer enough for me—when the meaning of words is not as clear as their sound—that is, when they do not offer to my thought objects as transparent in themselves as the terms that name them.

——

From the center we should perceive the circle.

——

One always adds a little of one's soul to what one thinks.

——

All gardeners live in beautiful places because they make them so.

——

Answer:—Those with whom one is happy without saying anything to them.

———

I have too much brain for my head. It cannot play comfortably in its box.

———

There must be several voices together in one voice for it to be beautiful. And several meanings in one word for it to be beautiful.

———

For in spite of ourselves we respect those whom we see respected.

———

It is through the flesh that we judge what is hard and what is soft.

———

Man loves what is small; and he loves what is big, through the same weakness.

———

If, when a stone falls, God helps it to fall.

———

That man has donkey's ears that don't show.

———

I have to oil my brain.

———

I stop when I see no more light; it is impossible for me to write by feeling my way.

———

——for wine is a wet fire.

1807

. . . all the pleasures it does not bless (religion).

———

Dream of the constellations that withdraw from the sky and set one after the other at sunrise. Beauty of the weather. Magnificence of this spectacle. Among the constellations, some set in the south and others in the north.

———

Why in language and in the course of all violent passions there is always something familiar and naive.

———

What is promised to you in dreams is given to you in dreams!

———

To translate well, art is needed, and much art.

———

Those who have judgment use it as much in judging stones as in judging men.

———

Beauty is something animal, the beautiful is something celestial.

———

To give color and shape to what is diaphanous, and always to give some transparence to what is opaque.—Transparent surfaces.

———

Thoughts still in seed: they must be left to develop. If we touch them, they will be spoiled.

———

When what we say is similar to what we are.

———

In living, one learns how to read. (How, and with what result.)

———

Little people have few passions, they hardly have anything but needs.

———

Chinese. This people dressed in silk.

———

The worker must have his hand on the work,—the thought must survive outside the mind,—and the words must clearly detach themselves from the paper.

    The worker must have his hand on the work: which means that he does not have to rely on explanations, notes, prefaces, etc. The thought must survive outside the mind: which means outside any systems or intentions of the author. And the words must clearly detach themselves from

the paper: which means that they can attach themselves easily to the reader's attention, his memory, that they be suitable for quotation, displacement. . . .

———

A woman without a belly, a mind without entrails, a
mummy who is alive and who moves.

———

Speak for the ear and write for the memory.

———

Small books are more durable than big ones; they go farther. The booksellers revere big books; readers like small
ones. An exquisite thing is worth more than a huge thing.
     A book that reveals a mind is worth more than one that
only reveals its subject.

———

——Like those clocks that ring the same hour twice.

———

Poetry of ideas.

———

Winter is more a time of piety. Religious holidays must
therefore be more numerous then.

———

Every composition has need of some repetition in its parts
to be well understood and retained by the memory and to
strike us as a whole. In all symmetry, there is a middle.
Every middle is the knot of a repetition, that is to say, of
two similar extremities.

———

Few minds are spacious; few even have an empty place in them or can offer some vacant point. Almost all have narrow capacities and are filled by some knowledge that blocks them up. What a torture to talk to filled heads, that allow nothing from the outside to enter them! A good mind, in order to enjoy itself and allow itself to enjoy others, always keeps itself larger than its own thoughts. And in order to do this, these thoughts must be given a pliant form, must be easily folded and unfolded, so that they are capable, finally, of maintaining a natural flexibility.

All those short-sighted minds see clearly within their little ideas and see nothing in those of others; they are like those bad eyes that see from close range what is obscure and cannot perceive what is clear from afar. Night minds, minds of darkness.

Great minds are those that disguise their limits, that mask their mediocrity.

During our youth, there is often something in us that is better than ourselves, I mean better than our desires, our pleasures, our yieldings, and our inclinations. Our soul is good then, even though our intelligence and will are not.

Painters say there are pictures in which there is no air. We also have poems with characters in which nothing is located, in which there is no space.

It is impossible to sing and dance correctly without pleasure, since the act of following all true measure is naturally agreeable. But the moral order also consists of measure and harmony, and it is equally impossible to live well without a very great secret pleasure.

———

It seems to me in fact that our good qualities are more *ourselves* than our faults. Whenever N is not good, it is because he is different from himself.

———

Whoever does not see his friends in a good light loves them little.
  To see in a good light.—Whoever does not see in a good light is a bad painter, a bad friend, a bad lover. Whoever does not see in a good light has not been able to lift his mind up to what is there or his heart to what is good.

———

Strength is not energy. Some writers have more muscles than talent.

———

But if you paint a false window, at least paint it closed. Your lie will be more sensible, will be smaller and will fool people better.
  A stupid lie is one that can never make itself believed.

———

Someone said (I read it this morning): "Happiness is a hermit." This would not have been said a hundred years ago. At that time one thought (to speak like Chateaubriand) that solitude was good only with God.

———

People of intelligence often treat business in the way ignorant people treat books: they understand nothing.

——

In language there are little words that no one has the slightest idea what to do with. M. de Fz uses them with great dex-
terity.

——

The first poets or writers made madmen wise. The last seek
to make wise men mad.

——

No, men are not born to know, but they are destined for it.

——

It is not through the head that men touch each other.

——

Excess and the *too much* are not the same thing. Excess is
worthless, the *too much* is often necessary.

——

Of those who want us to be wrong and those who want us
to be right.

——

This line (the line of beauty) must unfold without breaking
in our head, but it is not possible for the hand to trace it
without interruption and without stopping and starting
several times.

——

To want to express such subtle ideas faithfully is to want to
capture an object that endlessly escapes and reappears, that

shows itself only for a moment. You must wait, in spite of yourself, you must look.

————

When the last word is always the one that offers itself first, the work becomes difficult.

————

Heaven gave strength to my mind only for a time—and this time has passed.

————

All religions = all women.

————

Properly speaking, man inhabits only his head and his heart. All other places are vainly before his eyes, at his sides, and under his feet: he himself is not there at all.

————

Those for whom the world is not enough: saints, conquerors, poets, and all lovers of books.

————

A nail, to hang his thoughts on.

————

If you want property to be sacred, bring heaven into it. Nothing is sacred where God is not.

————

A dark point in his mind is as unbearable to him as a grain of sand in his eye.

1808

I am like Montaigne: "unsuited to continuous discourse."

——

Wicked people have nothing human about them except passions: they are almost their virtues.

——

There is in us a base of joy and contentment. If nothing disturbs this source, if it keeps its purity, if too much earth or sand does not fall into it . . . Otherwise, we feel its sweetness and refreshment and are watered by it only when it overflows.

——

To be tragic, misfortunes must be rare.

——

The truth! Only God sees it.

——

. . . Like those flashes of sharp light that suddenly enter a dark room.

——

——maxims, because what is isolated can be seen better.

——

In fact, goodness undoubtedly makes us better than morality.

——

To finish! What a word. We finish nothing when we stop, when we say we have come to the end.

——

What makes us look for a long time is that we do not look where we should or that we look where we should not. But how to look where we should when we do not even know what we are looking for? And this is what always happens when we compose and when we create. Fortunately, by straying in this fashion, we make more than one discovery, we have good encounters, and often are repaid for what we have looked for without finding by what we have found without looking for.

——

Reminiscence is an operation whereby the mind picks up the trail of its memories in order to find the memory it has lost.

——

Here I am outside civil things, in the pure region of Art.

——

(In a dream.) To unite matter to forms, which are the purest, the most beautiful, the truest things in nature. (Written at night, without being able to see.)

——

Dry, not like wood, but like bread. That is to say, dry, but nourishing, dry but not hard, not arid.

——

Necessity can make a doubtful action innocent, but it cannot make it commendable.

———

——and the pernicious habit of accepting pleasures without gratitude.

———

Poets—and the images of objects help them more than their presence.

———

To be the soul of a body, but not the head, that is a noble ambition.

———

Sloth waiting for inspiration.

———

The breath of the mind is attention.

———

The paper is patient, but the reader is not.

———

. . . have built their power with dead bodies.

———

Animals love the people who talk to them.

———

The republic of ants and the monarchy of bees.

———

If we exclude the idea of God, it is impossible to have an exact idea of virtue.

———

The great inconvenience of new books is that they prevent us from reading old books.

———

This philosophy perpetually concerned with what we must believe, and never with what we must do, nor what we must be.

———

Voltaire had the soul of a monkey and the mind of an angel.

———

Freedom. The freedom to do something well. There is no need of any other kind.
    Truths. The truths that teach us to act well and to live well. There is no need of any other kind.

———

Abuse of words, foundation of ideology.

———

The punishment of those who have loved women too much is to love them forever.

———

Because to think of God we do not need our brain.

———

Everything we can measure seems small.

———

The century felt it was making progress by falling into the precipice.

——

Mme de Sévigné said that "the pen always has a great part in what we write." And language in what we say.

——

——singularly able to enter the ideas of others without ever leaving his own.

——

Tenderness is the repose of passion.

1809

——because the sublime gives a useful pleasure.

——

Whoever consults the light within himself (it is in everyone) excels at judging the objects this light illumines.

——

The ellipsis, favorable to brevity, saves time and space.

——

Of those who lie to deceive, and of those who lie to persuade truth.

——

A work is perfectly finished only when nothing can be added to it and nothing taken away.

——

He must not only cultivate his friends, but cultivate his friendships within himself. They must be kept, cared for, watered.

——

In raising a child, we must think of his old age. (Or: In raising childhood, we must think of old age.)

——

There is a degree of bad health that makes us happy.

——

We always lose the friendship of those who lose our esteem.

——

——When we will have lost our mortality . . .

——

Because in fact reason leads man back to his instincts.

——

——and the pain of the soul: to expiate the pleasures of the body.

——

Of those who have a visible soul.

——

Everything that becomes a duty should become dear.

——

There is an infinity of things that one does well only through necessity.

——

The talkative person is someone who speaks more than he thinks. Someone who thinks a great deal and who talks a great deal is never considered a talkative person. The talkative man speaks from his mouth, the eloquent man speaks from his heart.

1810

All cries and all complaints exhale a vapor, and from this vapor a cloud is formed, and from these heaped-up clouds come thunder, storms, the inclemencies that destroy everything.

Let's go; and follow your mistake.

Anger, which purges resentment.

1811

The bad must be changed into the good, the incomplete must be finished, and what is twisted must be straightened.

——

Credulity forges more miracles than trickery could invent.

——

Nothing corrects a badly made mind. A sad and irritating truth that we learn late and after so many wasted efforts!

1812

To let the reader sometimes complete the symmetry between words and to do no more than suggest it.

———

In this painting of our life given to us by our memories, everything is moving and depends on our point of view.

———

Ash Wednesday.
　　The face. After the face, action. Between the two, attitudes. But before everything, the idea.

———

And the sun, and its rays. And if, instead of touching you with his glance, someone touched you with his eyes; and if with his fingertip instead of his cane; and if with his hand and not with his glove.

———

(Ætatis, ann. 58)
　　Never the mind without the soul.

———

For the soul the mind is a sort of organ, a sort of eye, of language, of hearing, and even a brain, a sort of megaphone, of telescope, of compass. And sometimes this organ acts all on its own.

———

Having found nothing worth more than emptiness, he leaves space vacant.

———

The ideas of eternity and space have something divine about them, but not those of pure duration and simple extension.

———

——This great player of human chess.

———

The world is a drop of air.

———

A falling stone is animated by a kind of passion. It shatters not because of its weight, but because of the attraction that animates it, and this is a quasi-spiritual thing.

———

When I had the strength, I did not have the patience. I have the patience today and I no longer have the power.

———

The child must live with the world before living with society; and he must love his parents before loving his teachers and comrades.

———

——and to destroy my memory by my presence.

———

. . . and, how in everything I say my affections always
come before my thoughts, and how I am still dominated
more by a love for justice than a love for truth,—which is
very inconvenient when one considers the objectivity
needed to explain oneself . . .
    (*Nota*. Marvejols.)

———

Reason is against, but experience is absolutely for—something that happens often, and then experience should decide
and have the upper hand.

———

These beautiful words of Chateaubriand: "This moderation . . . without which everything is a lie."

———

Fortunately, when he lacks reasons he also lacks words.

———

Poetry made with little matter: with leaves, with grains of
sand, with air, with nothings, etc.

———

Of those who have a muse and those who have only their
soul.

———

Of the friendship we have for an old man. We love him in
the way we love a fleeting thing. He is a ripened fruit that we
are waiting to see fall. It is like knowing someone in very
bad health. These words of Epictetus are easily applied to
him: —I saw what is fragile break.

———

India. A subject capable of providing a fine story and one that carries its poetry within itself. It concerns an unknown country, unknown men, unknown customs. We want the truth about it: fiction would spoil everything.

1813

Date locum irae. Let anger pass, make a place for it; do not impede its progress; do not disturb its development, give it the time it needs to die out, open a wide path for it.

———

Gray hair, mixture of strength and old age.

———

There are words agreeable to the eye (in the same way there are words agreeable to the ear). By a fortunate combination of the letters that form them or by the harmony of these letters. For each letter has its shape.

———

Silence.—Joys of silence.—Thoughts must be born from the soul and words from silence.—An attentive silence.

———

What I call "phosphorescent." Colored sounds.

———

In political institutions, almost everything we call an abuse was once a remedy.

———

This world, for the other.

——

"Leave behind endless hope and vast thoughts," says the poet. I no longer have vast thoughts.

——

What is clear should not be drawn out too much. These useless explanations, these endless examinations are a kind of long whiteness and lead to boredom. It is the uniformity of a wall, of a long piece of laundry.

——

In order to know men, something must be chanced. Who risks nothing of himself knows nothing.

——

To thank heaven when it gives us beautiful dreams.

——

——to dream of freshness. Who dreams of freshness feels it.

——

There are, following Plato's idea, souls that not only do not have wings but do not even have feet (for progress or consistency) or hands (for work).

——

Egregie fallitur. He is wrong, but nobly, intelligently, with grace, with spirit, with wisdom and much beauty.

——

You have put up limits in vain; we see space out there and run towards it. We would like to break through your bars.—Your *nec plus ultra* was written by pygmies.

——

There is a residue of wisdom (as there is a residue of madness); and in human wisdom this residue purified by old age
is perhaps the best thing we have.

———

To be pathetic when we cry, we must cry without wanting
to and without knowing it.

———

. . . draw the attention and hold onto it; also: satisfy it.

———

Half myself mocks the other half.

———

A frightening thing, which is perhaps true: "old men want
to survive."

———

The rightness of a certain tact. Everything depends on it.

———

You want to explain everything by the facts that are known
to you. But the facts that are not known to you? What do
they say?

———

Peoples that have overthrown geography (like winds,
storms, and torrents).

———

I can do something well only slowly and with great effort.
     Our moments of light are all moments of happiness.
When it is bright in our mind, the weather is good.

1814

Nothing is better than a justified enthusiasm.

———

What leads us astray in morality is an excessive love of
pleasure; and what stops us or holds us back in metaphysics
is a love of certainty.

———

Our thoughts are sometimes an image of the world, sometimes a product of our mind, and sometimes the result or
fabrication of our excited will. When they are an image of
the world, they paint the truth. If they are the simple product of our mind, they represent our mind and paint something else as well. But if they are the result or fabrication of
our will alone, they paint nothing true, nothing that can
give pleasure. They are bizarre traits, writer's caprices,
mere pen scratchings. . . .

———

More than once I have brought the cup of abundance to my
lips; but it is a water that has always escaped me. (Another
version: I have often brought to my lips the cup that holds
abundance; it is a water that has always escaped me.)

———

In painting, the pure idea. In sculpture, a real base clothed by an idea. In painting, shadow and idea; in sculpture, idea with a body, the idea incorporated and not simply represented. In sculpture, the expressed idea is all on the surface; in painting, it must be within. Beauty is hollowed out in painting; in sculpture it is in relief.

———

———like those birds that never perch on anything but the peaks of the highest trees, on the tips of shrubs.

———

The end of life is bitter.

———

Bourgeois old age as compared to the old age of the poor.

———

Almost all men prefer danger to fear. Some prefer death to danger and to pain. This is because fear, danger, and pain disturb reason. The horse throws himself into the precipice to escape the spur.

———

He did not know how to do anything with just a little; neither with few men nor with little money. But such was his power that he took money and men and no one dared refuse him.

———

There is in each man a divine part that is born with him, and a human and even animal part that grows with time. The first must be conserved and carefully cultivated within ourselves, the other thrives without help.

———

In literature, beauty must not be fabricated.

——

The gleam of the diamond in the pearls of the dew.

——

Let us look for our lights in our feelings. There is a warmth in them that contains many clarities.

——

To put the soul into physics and the body into metaphysics, if we want the first to be true and the second to be believable. For in the physical world everything happens from such subtle causes and in the metaphysical world everything that happens should be similar to what we see, etc. . . .

Remember that God gave us the power to imagine what our nature has not given us the possibility of seeing.

——

Fire, ignition, and brightness; the body, its shadow and penumbra; sound, echo, and half-echo: everything has some shadow, some glow or reverberation. (Reflection.)

——

Neither in the arts, nor in logic, nor in life should an idea in any way be treated as a thing.

——

There is nothing perfectly true for man; I mean in human opinions. Just as there is nothing perfectly round.

——

If it concerns an individual, there is no cause for abstraction.
What is collective necessitates it, because every multitude
forms a whole only through fiction.

——

——for I have a very loving head and a stubborn heart.
Everything I admire is dear to me; and nothing that is dear
to me can ever become completely indifferent to me.

——

Our life is of woven wind.

——

To speak to God of everything; to dare to question him and
to be attentive to what he says about everything. But sometimes we take our own voice for that of God.

——

Sonorous prose. Is this an advantage or a drawback?

——

Courage (in a soldier) is maintained by a certain anger; anger is a little blind and likes to strike out. And from this follow a thousand abuses, a thousand evils and misfortunes
that are impossible to predict in an army during a war.

——

Retreat often into your sphere, rest yourself in your center,
plunge yourself into your element: good advice, which
must be remembered.

——

Of the sincerity of things. To see it. Truth consists of this.

1815

I confess that I am like an aeolian harp—which gives off
some pretty sounds but can play no songs.

———

Too much harmony. Prose can have too much of it; also too
much sweetness. And this is a very seductive fault, at first
very agreeable, but unbearable and ridiculous over the long
term.
    Varnish (in style) makes a glaze (for the reader).

———

Tormented by the cursed ambition always to put a whole
book in a page, a whole page in a sentence, and this sentence
in a word. I am speaking of myself.

———

As the hands would feel it or the eye would see it; that is the
great question.

———

Yes, light. But what does it shine on? It is beautiful even
when it shines on nothing. And when it shines on evil? Even
then it is beautiful; even if it shines on what is hideous.

———

Of the freedom of thoughts (and the freedom of words) in
the development of a text. And how (or through what art,
what practice, what turns of phrase) to keep the freedom
of thoughts and words, to keep their detached and mobile
air in the most easily followed and best constructed texts.
Nothing nailed down: let us make these words a guiding principle.

——

I do not like philosophy (and especially metaphysics) that is
four-legged or two-legged;—I want it to be winged and
singing.
     Let metaphysics therefore have wings.

——

You go to truth by way of poetry and I come to poetry by
way of truth.

——

——always occupied with the duties of others, never his
own, alas!

——

What is pleasing always has something chanced about it.

——

To write his views or his observations, his ideas, but not
his judgments. Our judgments limit our views of things.
Some enclosures, but no walls. The man who always writes
his judgments places before his eyes the *calpe* and the *abyla*.
He goes no farther and creates a *nec plus ultra*. Thus, in the
study of wisdom, many views and few judgments.

——

Of light. Dry light, wet light, warm light. (It is less clear, but it has much more effect.) Cold light. This is the light of artificial elegance, which comes from an ability without genius and a taste without enthusiasm.

Lafontaine: His taste is never without enthusiasm; nor that of Fontanes either, in those verses he has written in spite of himself.

———

Beyond domestic affections, all long-term feelings are impossible for the French.

———

When laws ruin customs . . .

———

Without fixed ideas, no fixed feelings.

———

When we find what we have been looking for, we don't have time to say it. We must die.

———

All foods are in fact good for someone who is hungry, but not for someone who has no appetite.

———

Leave dreams of the imagination time to evaporate.

———

To seek that style which makes one perceive or discover more meanings than it explains.

———

It is probable that the eye of the bird takes pleasure in colors (those of flowers), in greenery, and even in the sparkling of water.

——

One must die lovable (if one can).

——

Reason does not reason. It goes straight to the fact or the consequence.

——

That: we cannot escape certain errors except from above, that is to say, in raising our mind above human things.— Through the roof or through what is high; through the window or through the wall; through the door or through ordinary solutions.

——

When a truth is better conceived through abstraction, use the abstraction; if not, don't.

——

France destroyed by its philosophers.

——

It is not light that burns, that purifies, that consumes, that divides, and that recomposes: it is fire. And this fire we are talking about always follows light.

——

Of what must be said and what must not be said. The importance of knowing.

——

Old age and its mask.

———

Everything is new. And we are living among events so singular that old people have no more knowledge of them, are no more habituated to them, and have no more experience of them than young people.

We are all novices, because everything is new.

———

When you no longer love what is beautiful, you can no longer write.

———

In such times, if you want neither to lie nor to wound, you are reduced to being silent.

———

When everything becomes unbearable . . . That is the rule. Then necessity makes the law, or changes it.

1816

Plato. The poetic spirit that gives life to the languors of his dialectic. He is lost in the void; but we can see his wings beating, we can hear their noise. His imitators lack these wings.

———

A symmetry that everywhere makes itself felt and does not show itself.

———

These simple foods. For it is not enough to live (or to eat them) with pleasure, but with joy.

1817

Melancholy: when we have sorrows without a name.

——

It is better to be concerned with being than with nothingness. Dream therefore of what you still have rather than of
what you have lost.

——

God! . . . Always! always! Never—never—

1818

. . . to procure for himself a moment of beauty.

———

". . . What is involuntary in human nature." This "involuntary" is very true, very beautiful, very well observed; and this observation is new.

———

The two suns we have in our head.

———

You want to talk to someone: first open your ears.

———

I am an aeolian harp. No wind has passed through me.

———

Madness is an illness of the brain, not of the mind.

———

Then, God withdrew his forces into himself, and we grew old.

———

Luminous words, like those drops of light we see in fire-
works.

––––

If you want to think well, to write well, to act well, first
make a "place" for yourself, a "true place." Because we lack
true places, we put our thoughts outside the true light and
our conduct outside order.

––––

These heads in which all lights have been extinguished, like
these lanterns . . .

1819

Happy is the man who can do only one thing: in doing it, he fulfills his destiny.

———

Of the silence and darkness that surround the laws.

———

Don Quixote going to Tobosa and talking to Sancho as Socrates did to his disciples; and this is not ridiculous and does not even seem out of place.

———

Because they know all the words, they think they know all the truths.

———

There are things we can speak of only in writing, that we cannot know except when thinking of writing them down, and that we cannot, however, think of writing except when we know them in advance.

1821

And the most terrible, the most horrible of catastrophes imaginable, the conflagration of the universe, can it be anything more than the crackling, the burst, and the evaporation of a grain of powder on a candle?

———

God will draw in his breath and the whole world will disappear. No more theater, no more actors, no more spectators; smoke, and the smoke of a breath, the warmth of a breath.

1823

And perhaps there is no advice to give a writer more important than this: —Never write anything that does not give you great pleasure.

———

Spaces . . . I would almost say . . . imaginary, existence is so much in them, etc.

1824

Nota.— The true—the beautiful = the just—the holy—

Afterword

I. AN AUTHOR WITHOUT A BOOK, A WRITER WITHOUT WRITINGS

That we think of Joubert as a writer close to us, closer than the great literary figures of his time, cannot be accounted for simply by the obscurity, the distinguished obscurity, in which he lived, died, and then lived on. It is not enough to be a faintly illuminated name in one's lifetime to shine, as Stendhal hoped to do, a century or two later. It is not even enough for a great work to be great and stand out on its own for posterity to recognize it one day and put it back into the brilliance of broad daylight. It may be that one day mankind will know everything—people, truths, and worlds— but there will always be some work of art—or perhaps all of art— that will fall outside this universal knowledge. That is the privilege of artistic activity: what it produces must often remain unknown even to a god.

It is still true that many works are prematurely exhausted from having been admired too much. The great blaze of glory that makes writers and artists so happy as they grow old and that burns brightest at their death consumes a substance in them that will thenceforth be missing from their work. The young Valéry sought out in every famous book the flaw that made it known: an aristocrat's judgment. But one often has the feeling that death will at last bring silence and calm to the work that has been left to itself. During his lifetime, even the most detached and indifferent writer is still fighting for his books. He is alive, and that is enough; he stands behind them because of the life that remains in him and that he gives to them. But his death, even if it goes unnoticed, restores the secret and shuts up the thought again. Now that the thought is alone, will it unfold or close in on itself, destroy or fulfill itself, find or lose itself? And will it ever be alone? Even oblivion does not always reward those who seem to have deserved it through their gift of great discretion.

Joubert had this gift. He never wrote a book. He only prepared to write one, resolutely seeking the exact conditions that would allow him to write it. Then he forgot even this plan. More precisely, what he was seeking—this source of writing, this space in which to write, this light to circumscribe in space—demanded of him, affirmed in him inclinations that made him unfit for all ordinary literary work, or made him turn away from it. In this he was one of the first completely modern writers, preferring the center to the sphere, sacrificing results to the discovery of their conditions, and writing not in order to add one book to another but to take command of the point from which it seemed to him all books issued, the point which, once it was found, would relieve him of the need to write any books.

It would be doing Joubert an injustice, however, to attribute such a thought to him as though it were his clear intention, single-mindedly pursued, when he only discovered it little by little, often lost it and obscured it, and could only sustain it later by transforming it into wisdom. That is why it is so easy to mistake him for one of those moralists for whose sake Nietzsche loved French literature. Almost all his editors, even recent ones, have presented the reflections of his *Notebooks* in sententious arrangements and under general titles borrowed from the emptiest and vaguest of philosophies—family and society; wisdom and virtue; truth and error; life and death; literary judgments—and have thereby encouraged misunderstanding and failed to recognize what was essentially new and even ahead of its time in his quest: the progress of a thought that does not yet think or of a language of poetry that attempts to return to itself.

Joubert is not Chamfort, or Vauvenargues, or La Rochefoucauld. He does not make brief thoughts into witty remarks. He does not coin a philosophy. He does not assume, with concise formulas, that abrupt declarative power used by the lofty, sceptical, and bitter moralists to make their doubt categorical. What he wrote, he wrote almost every day, dating it and giving it no other reference than this date, no other perspective than the movement of the days that brought it to him. This is how he must be read.

This perspective changes everything. To the same extent that the many collections of Joubert's *Thoughts* seem to display a precious, wary, but indifferent wisdom, the *Notebooks*, as they were written over the course of an entire lifetime and as they have been restored to us—emerging from this hazard, this pressure of life—are passionate reading, carrying us along in their hazardous movement towards an end that is only revealed at rare moments, in the brief rift of a clearing.

The story we have here is formed of the deepest intimacy, the search for that intimacy, for the path by which to attain it and the space of words with which it must finally merge. "And everything comes from the entrails, everything, even the least expression. This is perhaps inconvenient, but necessary: I submit to it." Joubert suffered from this necessity. He would have liked not to be one of "those minds that submerge themselves or penetrate too far ahead into what they are thinking," a fault which is, he says, that of his century, but a privileged fault: he only seeks, sometimes, to preserve its language. Then one day he has to observe sadly: "I have no more surface." Which, for a man who wants to write, who certainly cannot write except through art, through contact with images and through the space with which they put him in contact, is a painful statement. How to speak from depth alone, in that state of submersion in which everything is arduous, harsh, irregular? An interior thing, a thing submerged. "When one paints an interior thing, one is painting a thing submerged. And submersion, however well illuminated it may be, can never present the uniform and vivid brightness of a surface." And Joubert loves that surface brightness, and he will not stop trying to imagine as another surface, endlessly added to itself, that great depth to which he descends, to which he rises.

In this journal, there are few details that touch on what we call private life or public life, and yet now and then there are discreet allusions that still have a certain evocative force. In 1801: "This young man you call Bonaparte." Upon the death of his mother: "At ten o'clock this evening, my poor mother! My poor mother!" In January: "The white markings of the snow, here and there scattered on the greenness in time of thaw." In May, in Hyères: "The cool during summer." In October: "The cry of the chimney

sweep; the song of the cricket." Sometimes, rough drafts of
thoughts that are still involved with circumstances: "Pleasure of
being seen from afar." "The occupation of watching time pass."
Or images of a kind, steeped in their secret source: "The black
hair in the grave." "The shifting path of the water. . . . A river of
air and of light. . . . Folds of clarity. . . . And it is from this point
on the earth that my soul takes flight." He also talks about himself,
not about what he is doing or about what happens to him, but
about what is deep inside him, about the demands of his mind
and, behind his mind, of what he calls his soul. An intimacy that is
yet barely his own, that always remains at a distance from him and
at a distance from this distance, forcing him often to observe himself in the third person and, after he has noted that "I do not have a
patient mind," to correct himself immediately with: "He does not
have. . . ." Still more rare—though there are many brief but precise notes on his health, which continually preoccupied him—are
the words of anguish when he seems to approach his limits, this
man who finds it necessary always to stop his mind short of its
boundaries in order to prevent it from being bounded; and the
brief lines that arrest us: "I have no more vast thoughts," ". . . incapable of writing," "(Worn out)." That last, in parentheses,
shortly before his death.

Why Didn't He Write?

Why didn't Joubert write books? Early in his life he is attentive
only to what is written, interested only in writing. As a young
man, he is close to Diderot; a little later, close to Restif de la Bretonne, both prolific men of letters. In middle age, his best friends
are famous writers, with whom he lives a literary life and who,
knowing his incomparable talent for thought and form, also
gently goad him out of his silence. Beyond that, he is in no way a
man paralyzed by difficulties of expression: his numerous and ex-
tensive letters are written with that aptitude for writing that is in
some sense the gift of his century and to which he adds witty nu-
ances and embellishments of phrasing that show he is always
happy to talk and happy in words. Yet this extremely capable
man, who writes almost every day in a notebook he has near him,

does not publish anything and leaves nothing to be published. (At least according to the customs of his time: even when Chateaubriand publishes a few of his thoughts after his death, the edition is a private one limited to his friends. In our day, he might not have resisted outside solicitations, any more than Valéry resisted Gide. Fontanes wrote him in 1803: "I urge you to write down your day's meditations every evening when you come home. After some time you will choose among these fancies of your thought, and you will be surprised to see that almost without knowing it you have made a very beautiful work." It is to Joubert's credit that he refused to make this very beautiful work.)

We could respond by saying that he is one of those writers whose journal makes them sterile by giving the pleasure of a false abundance, the pleasure of an appearance of words in which they can revel without restraint. But nothing could be more alien to him. Though his journal is still built upon the days, it is not a reflection of them, it reaches toward something other than them. Besides, it is fairly late in his life that the *Notebooks* become a real habit for him, and even later that they take on the importance and direction that, through the great variety of his reflections, assert the constancy of his preoccupation. It certainly seems that until the age of forty he feels he is about to produce beautiful writings in the way so many others have done: on Universal Goodwill, on Pigalle, on Cook, even a novel—projects of which we still have some fragments. So, in the beginning no *Notebooks* or few; they impose themselves on him only when he begins to *think* of writing and when he recognizes that this thought is his vocation, is the attraction he must submit to, the act by which he will fulfill himself, sometimes in a melancholy way, with regret at not having "told everything," but also without regret, sure of his priorities and of not having failed them.

"But in fact what is my art? . . . What end does it propose? What does it produce? What does it give birth to and make exist? What do I pretend to do and what do I want to do in doing it? Is it writing in general, to assure myself of being read? The one ambition of so many people! Is that what I want? . . . This must be examined attentively, at great length, until I know the answer." That was written on October 22, 1799; Joubert was forty-five. A

year later, on October 27: "When? you say. I answer you:—When
I have circumscribed my sphere." That question is pursued day
after day, month after month, year after year, throughout his entire life, but we would be wrong to regard him as another Amiel,
exhausting himself in self-scrutiny. He is admirably aware—one
of the first to know—that the impulse he must respond to is an
impulse about which reasoning is insufficient and dangerous,
about which it is not even right to say true things, because it is in
some sense outside of strict truth, challenging that part of illusion
and that environment of the imaginary that hard and fast reason
does not have to take into account. Joubert, who seems to draft
only quite abstract reflections, nevertheless has no doubt that as
an author without a book and a writer without writings, he is already purely dependent on art. "Here I am outside civil things, in
the pure region of Art." He has his moments of doubt, but what is
most striking is the confidence of his progress and the certainty
that even if he doesn't answer his friends' question, "What?", by
any visible work, he is occupied by something more essential and
that concerns art more essentially than it concerns a work.*

Then what is he occupied by? Perhaps he wouldn't like anyone to be able to say that he knows. What he knows is that he is
seeking what he does not know and that this is the source of the
difficulty of his search and the happiness of his discoveries: "But
how to look where we should when we don't even know what
we are looking for? And this is what always happens when we
compose and when we create. Fortunately, by straying in this fashion, we make more than one discovery, we have good encounters. . . ." We often feel that if he has a work in mind at these
times, it is really for the purpose of using this ordinary plan to en-
velop and hide, even from his own eyes, the more secret plan, the
one that is difficult to grasp and to express, the one that he feels
burdened with—an almost mythical work that is alluded to now
and then and whose nature is such, he says, "that even the name of
the subject must not be in the title." After which he adds: "I will
title it: 'On Man.' " Or he answers the reproaches directed at him
by his friends or perhaps by his productive mind. The reproach

*"It is necessary to resemble art without resembling any work."

that he lacks variety and is only interested in one thing: "If he turns in the same circle? It's the horizon of his subject. Add: the circle of immensity." The reproach that he doesn't know how to conclude: "To finish! What a word. We finish nothing when we stop and when we say we have come to the end." The reproach, a more serious one, of having finished before any beginning: "When the last word is always the one that offers itself first, the work becomes difficult." The difficulty of providing his "ideas" with a lodging worthy of them, composed of their freedom itself, respecting and preserving in them their simplicity of image, their aspect of invisibility and their refusal to associate with one another as reasons: "My ideas! It is the house for lodging them that costs me so much to build."

To Translate Things in Space

A work whose subject is quite other than the manifest subject, that must not be concluded and cannot begin, a work that in some sense fails in relation to itself, at a distance from what it expresses and so that what it expresses opens out in that distance, is laid down there, is preserved there and finally disappears there. In 1812—he is nearly sixty—here is the name he gives that "house" which, seven years before, cost him such effort to build: "Having found nothing worth more than emptiness, he leaves space vacant." On the threshold of old age, is this an admission that he is giving up, the confession of failure to which his excessive demands have led him? It may not be a declaration of triumph, but everything shows that he in no way regards it as negative and that if he resigns himself to it, it is because he prefers to stand rigorously by this discovery rather than develop it with approximations that would betray it. *Space*—this is, really, the core of his experience, what he finds when he thinks about writing, what he finds close to all writing, the marvel of intimacy that makes literary expression at once a thought and the echo of that thought (which is to say, for him, not a weakened thought, but one that is more profound, being more tenuous, though redoubled, more remote, closer to that remoteness it designates and from which it flows); turned at once toward that reservoir of ease and indeterminateness that is in us and that is our soul, and toward that web of light, air, and infinity that is above us and that is the sky and that is God.

It is hard to say what was the starting point for this "experience" of Joubert's. In a way, he always thinks everything at once, especially since he has to express himself in isolated thoughts, as though he did not exist in the intervals between them. And yet it certainly seems that someone who could write in his early maturity: "The poets should be the great subject of study of the philosopher who wants to know man," has taken first of all from poetry and more precisely from the strangeness of literary writing the surprise of what he will have to think all his life, the sphere whose form will be adopted henceforth by his most varied reflections on man, natural philosophy, cosmology, or theology, even as they help keep this sphere in motion. When he notes that ". . . to represent with air, to circumscribe in a small space great voids or great plenums, no, immensity itself and all of matter, these are the wonders, incontestable and easy to verify, that are perpetually brought about through the word and through writing," he is designating, still in a confused way but already with confidence, the point to which he will keep returning: the power to represent through absence and to manifest through remoteness, a power that lies at the center of art, that seems to move things away in order to say them, to keep them at a remove so that they may become clear, a power of transformation, of translation, in which it is this very removal (space) that transforms and translates, that makes invisible things visible, that makes visible things transparent, that thus makes itself visible in them and then discovers itself to be the luminous depth of invisibility and irreality from which everything comes and in which everything is concluded.

A surprising experience that sometimes seems to us nearly to merge with Rilke's, that is also in some sense an anticipation of Mallarmé's pursuit, though as soon as one tries to look at the two of them together, Joubert's experience diverges from Mallarmé's all the more distinctly because it comes close to it, and these slight differences may enlighten us about the centers of gravity of the one and the other.

2. AN EARLY VERSION OF MALLARMÉ

Georges Poulet, speaking of Joubert in one of his best essays, has recalled Mallarmé's poetic experience, which Joubert's thought really does direct us toward quite often.* And between the two figures, how many connections: the same discretion, a sort of fading away of the person, the rarity of inspiration, but all the force of that apparent weakness and a great rigor in the pursuit, a lucid obstinacy in striving toward the unknown end, an extreme attention to words, to their form, to their essence and, finally, the feeling that literature and poetry are the locus of a secret that should perhaps be put before everything else, even the glory of making books. From time to time, in one phrase or another of the *Notebooks*, it is almost Mallarmé's voice that we imagine we hear. On June 8, 1823, less than a year before his death: "Spaces . . . I would almost say . . . imaginary, existence is so much in them, etc." No doubt Mallarmé would have stopped at "imaginary," but isn't this already him talking, with this suspended utterance, these silences that shape the air and this way of holding back the word so that it may break free and rise up, of itself, to its point of manifestness? This is troubling.

What matters to us, however, in this anticipated presence of Mallarmé, is that such a close resemblance between the two figures and between the two thoughts forces us to regard them primarily in the light of what distinguishes them, and to ask ourselves why such closely related meditations, the intuition of the same routes, the appeal of the same images, lead them so far from each other. The points of departure are almost the same. Both of them have a profound sense of the "distance" and the "separation" that alone allow us to speak, imagine, and think. Both of them feel that the force of poetic communication does not come from the fact that it immediately makes us take part in things, but that it gives them to us beyond their reach. Only Joubert, a less exclusive spirit and perhaps lacking certain of the demands that make Mallarmé a poet, has not separated the two regions: on the contrary, in this separation—this web of absence and void that he calls space—he has seen the common part of the things, the

*Georges Poulet, *The Interior Distance*. Poulet also emphasizes their differences.

words, the thoughts and the worlds, this sky above and this transparency in us, that here and there form a pure expanse of light. When he discovers that in literature all things are spoken, are made to be seen, are revealed with their true form and their secret measure as soon as they are distanced, spaced apart, attenuated, and finally unfurled in the uncircumscribed and indeterminate void to which the imagination is one of the keys, he boldly concludes from this that this void and this absence are the very foundation of the most material realities, to such an extent, he says, that if one were to squeeze the world to force the void out of it, it would not fill one's hand.

Through the Distance and Through the Void

"This globe is a drop of water; the world is a drop of air. Marble is thickened air." "Yes, the world is made of gas, and even of a clear gas. Newton calculated that the diamond had (. . .) times more hollow space than solidity, and the diamond is the most compact of bodies." "With its gravitations, its impenetrabilities, and all those blind forces that scholars make so much noise about, . . . what is all matter but a grain of metal scooped out, a speck of glass hollowed out, a well-blown bubble of water filled with the play of light and shade; a shadow, in fact, in which nothing weighs except on itself, nothing is impenetrable except (for) itself. . . ." In Joubert there is an entire natural philosophy and cosmology of dreaming (not, perhaps, very remote from the assertions of a more modern scholarship) that he ventures into, driven by the need to reconcile the real and the imaginary, and that tend less to deny the reality of things than to make them exist from almost nothing—an atom of air, a spark of light or even no more than the emptiness of the place they occupy: "Observe that everywhere and in everything, what is delicate carries what is compact, and what is light holds suspended all that is heavy." And so it is clear why poetic speech can evoke things and, by translating them in space, make them manifest through their distance and their emptiness: this distance inhabits them, this emptiness is already in them, it is right to grasp them through it, and the vocation of words is to extract in some sense the invisible center of their true signification. One approaches the body through the shadow, through the penumbra of this shadow, and when one has arrived at the oscillating limit where it does not fade but is fringed and penetrated with light. But for the word to reach this limit and represent it, it too must naturally become "a drop of light," and be the image of what it designates, an image of itself and of the imaginary, in order finally to merge with the indeterminate extent of space, at the same time that it lifts to the roundness of a perfect sphere the moment that it bears within itself, in its own extreme lightness, and that it defines, by its own transparency.

"Transparency, diaphanousness, meagerness of substance, magic; the imitation of the divine that has made all these things with little, and so to speak, with nothing: this is one of the essential characteristics of poetry." "In our written language, there must be voice, soul, space, open air, words that continue to exist on their own, and that carry their place with them." "The force of communication. . . . It is a subtle, fine force whose existence makes itself felt and does not show itself. Like that of ether in electricity." "A poetic vapor, a cloud that is resolved in prose."

However ethereal language must become for him, we have to point out that Joubert never invested it with the power of negation—passing into, through, and toward nothingness—which poetry obliged Mallarmé to explore. If the modesty of the word establishes a distance between us and things, a distance without which we would be exposed to the muteness of suffocation, it does this not by *negating* things but by opening them and, because of this opening, by setting free the portion of light and the interval that constitute them; or again, it does this by making palpable what is beyond the body, by consenting to that *beyond* through which every body affirms itself, by admitting that fore-body which is "the secret extension of its substance." The word does not negate, but consents, and if it sometimes appears to be conspiring with nothingness, this "nothingness," says Joubert, is none other than "the invisible plenitude of the world," evidence of which is brought to light by speech, an emptiness that does not show itself but is a luminous presence, a fissure through which invisibility blossoms.

Around 1804, first under the influence of Malebranche, because of the resemblance he perceived between that philosopher's language and his own, and then again because of the extension of his literary experience into a religious experience, and having taken as far as he could the evisceration of things and the hollowing of the real, Joubert found in God the end and the resting place of that emptiness and made him the space of space, as others had made him the thought of thought. It would be easy to decide that here the name of God comes in conveniently to stop up the great hole that, in his desire for lightness and clearing, he has finally recognized and established in all things. Without this name, or if it were only a name, wouldn't everything fall back into the nothingness that it touches, tames, and savors as the ineffable contact of every visible and invisible certainty? This could well be. But let us accept his experience as he felt it and represented it. What we then have to point out in order to judge it correctly is that he has such a strong sense of the impalpable, and such a sure understanding of that emptiness he calls space, that he never seems to fear that everything will scatter in it or be annihilated by it. The immensity of space, as Georges Poulet notes quite rightly, is not a source of anguish for him, as it was for Pascal, but of the exaltation of a calm joy, and if God comes to him, it is not as the end of a chain of reasons, but as the full extent of that joy—of which God will then become the single object.

The Book, The Sky

During his nights of insomnia, Joubert goes out and contemplates the sky. "*Insomni nocte.*" "Insomnia, 5 o'clock in the morning."* What do these nocturnal reflections give to him? The very thing that is inside him, but realized outside: that supreme book that it seems he will never write, and that he is writing in some sense without knowing it, by *thinking* about writing it. Up above, there is space and at distant intervals a condensation of space into light, a unified and orderly solitude of points, each of which seems unaware of the others, even though with certain of them it composes some figure one can vaguely perceive and with all of them the unfigurable whole of their dispersion. The stars are pleasing to Joubert, but more than the stars, which often sparkle

---

*This kind of contemplation, however, only takes place in the month of August. Joubert, a chilly genius, does not go out and meditate in winter.

too brightly, he likes the great radiating space, the diffuse light that is slowly revealed there and slowly reveals that easy simultaneity of different perfections, the composition of what is vague and what is precise. In a note written in his early middle age, we see him trying to form for himself a cosmology quite close to that of Cyrano de Bergerac and the ancient authors, in which the stars are only holes in the sky, voids through which the enigma of a hidden light gathers and pours out: hollows in space, space no longer condensed but subtracted and diminished to the point of rupture, when it becomes brightness.

These metaphorical contemplations that refer us to nocturnal space as to a great text of silences, and to the book as to an unmoving sky of stars in motion, may appear to be within anyone's reach, but they open on Joubert as the exacting expression of what he must accomplish.* A model of ambition that nevertheless does not crush this modest genius, because what is written up there guarantees him that he can represent it through art, if it is true that when we are withdrawn from ourselves we find in us the same intimacy of space and light, an intimacy which we must henceforth take great pains with so that our life may correspond to it, our thought preserve it and our works make it visible.

". . . And all my stars in a sky. . . . All space is my canvas. Stars fall to me from the mind."

It would be tempting and glorious for Joubert, to imagine we see in him a first untranscribed edition of that *Coup de dés* which, said Valéry the day he was initiated into the secret thoughts of Mallarmé, "at last" elevated "one page to the power of the starry sky." And we can sense similar demands behind the dreams of Joubert and the work realized a century later: in Joubert as in Mallarmé the desire to substitute for ordinary reading, in which one must go from part to part, the spectacle of a simultaneous speech in which everything would be said at once, without confusion, in one "flash, complete, peaceful, intimate and in the end uniform."† Which presupposes both a thinking quite different from that of the reasoners who make their way from proof to proof,

---

*"August 1 (*insomni nocte*). I would like thoughts to succeed one another in a book like stars in the sky, with order, with harmony, but effortlessly and at intervals, without touching, without mingling. . . ."
†*Notebooks*, February 7, 1805.

and also a language quite different from the language of discourse (essential preoccupations of the author of the *Notebooks*). It also presupposes more profoundly the encounter with or the creation of that space of vacancy in which, no particular thing coming to break the infinite, everything is there, in some sense present in the nullity, *place in which nothing will take place but the place*: ultimate goal of these two minds.

But the similarity of purpose ends here. Even looking at it only from the outside, the poem, in the immobility of its affirmation, is subject to a prodigious movement that Joubert did everything to escape from: movements of "withdrawal," of "prolongation," of "flight," movements that speed up and slow down, divide and superimpose through an increasing animation all the more painful to the mind in that it does not progress, does not develop, and rejecting the relief of succession, obliges us to endure at once, in an effect that is massive even though it is spaced out, every form of movement's uneasiness. Nothing could strike a more serious blow at Joubert's spiritual aim than this burgeoning in the heart of absence, this infinitely repeated coming and going that is the emptiness of indeterminate space.

Undoubtedly, in *Un Coup de dés* as in the sky, there is a secret order that Joubert could accept, but this order imitates chance, claims to enter into the intimacy of the game of chance, perhaps in order to fathom its rules, perhaps in order to carry the rigor of words and the precision of thoughts to the point at which the determined extreme can integrate indetermination. Undoubtedly, in that sky which is the poem, there is the still future and always uncertain flash of the "constellation" that the poem will perhaps also be, at the height of possibility. But Joubert would never be able to accept the preceding devastation in which it is necessary that nothing be given in order that something else *be*, something purer than what is. He would never regard as a descent toward "the identical neutrality of the abyss" the movement of nonrealization through which, in all things, we search for a void in order to find light.

Even the word *chance* is foreign to him. And the dramatic conjunction of the throw of the dice and chance would seem to him incapable of representing thought at the level where it en-

counters poetry. It is here, actually, that his reflection is most un-
shakable. Joubert insists that thought not be determined, the way
reason can be determined. He insists that it be raised above the
constraint of reasonings and proofs, that it be finite thought that
begins in the infinite, just as he insists that poetic speech, in the
perfection of its completeness, hold and uphold the vagueness,
the duplicity and the ambiguity of several meanings, the better
to represent the intermeaning and the beyond-meaning toward
which it is always oriented. But this indetermination is not chance.
Chance refers to that very vain and very apparent part of reality
which reason—satisfied only with proofs and intent on reducing
everything to accounts—tries to control through calculation.*
The space Joubert arrives at is without chance and without de-
termination, and literature, which is space that has become the
power to communicate, is that sky arranged with stars in which
the infinity of the sky is present in each star and in which the infi-
niteness of the stars is not troubling but makes tangible the freedom of the infinitely empty expanse.

Such is the firm contradiction that he sees harmoniously resolved above, that he himself runs up against, and that will not re-
duce him to silence but will deflect him from any finished work. It
is to his credit that he at once recognized in art and poetry a mode
of affirmation incapable of being too much mediated by reason or
claimed by too immediate a sensibility. He senses in poetry and art
a quite different possibility that he will try all his life to clarify: a
need for relations that are even more rigorous than those of reason
but that are pure, light, and free; a more intense contact with profound intimacy than the contact of sensibility, and yet from a distance, for what is intimately touched by this single point is the distance itself experienced as our intimacy and the remoteness in us
experienced as our center. Relations, therefore, that elude what-
ever temporal regularity exists in the logical relations of reason
but that also elude the instantaneous shocks of tangible presence:
the communication, at a distance and through distance, of the immediate; the finite and in some sense punctual affirmation of the
infinite immensity.

*"Newton. He was gifted with the faculty of knowing the 'how much' in all
things." "The only thing Newton invented was the how much."

But how to go from the sky to the star, from the poem—an unlimited web of space—to the pure and single word in which it must come together, from the beautiful that is undetermined to the rigor of the perfection of the beautiful?* More than the solutions that Joubert sometimes proposes,† it is the care he always takes not to ignore the contrary needs of these two movements, even at the expense of himself, that makes him important and sometimes exemplary. He apparently failed. But he preferred that failure to the compromise of success. Being beyond any plan to realize anything, he certainly suffered a great deal from his commitment to *intermittency*, which he clearly sees as the *continuous* depth of the soul, but which he has to experience, within himself, as a cessation of the mind, a painful interruption of all power, a fall into nothingness and no longer into the beautiful silent void. He rarely confided in anyone, but we know of some instances (mainly in letters: to Mole, to Fontanes, to Mme de Vintimille). And the *Notebooks* accumulated images through which he tried to reconcile himself to his difficulties: "I confess that I am like an aeolian harp—which gives off some beautiful sounds but can play no songs." "I am an aeolian harp. No wind has passed through me." The aeolian harp: we can see why he takes this image from the ossianic mode, for it is as though space itself has become instrument and music—an instrument with all the extent and continuity of open space, but music composed of sounds that are always discontinuous, disjointed, and unfettered. Elsewhere, he explains the gaps in his meditation and the white spaces that interrupt his phrases by the tension he has to maintain in his strings so as to resonate properly, by the slackening that results from this harmony and by the long period of time he needs to "recover his strength and tighten himself again."

---

*"Everything that is beautiful is undetermined." "It is always what terminates or limits a thing that forms its character, its precision, its neatness, its perfection."
†One being music, the solution that the Symbolists would delude themselves with. "Thoughts must follow one another and be connected to one another like sounds in music, through their relationships alone—harmony—and not like links in a chain." In a moving but naive way, Joubert mourns the unknown thoughts he would have had through expression in painting or in music: "Ah! if I could express myself through music, through dance, through painting, as I express myself through words, how many ideas I would have that I do not have and how many feelings that will be forever unknown to me."

This collaboration of time, this conjunction, necessary if he is to write, of the space within and the space without—this is what has led him to think only within the framework of a journal, relying on the movement of the days and demanding from that movement the passage from himself to himself—to the expression of himself; and he is the patient, often disappointed anticipation of this expression, just as the harp is the silent anticipation of the wind. Responding once again to his friends' impatience, he finds this new reason for his delay: ". . . And I must also let my clouds pile up and condense." This is clearly the problem of the sky and the star, the great enigma of the *Coup de dés* which must be at once the identical neutrality of the abyss, the high vacancy of the sky and the constellation that is cast up there, at the height of a "perhaps." And for the clouds to pile up and condense, time is needed, a two-fold labor of transformation through time: first, time must transmute events and impressions into the remoteness of memory (and Joubert says: "One should not express oneself as one feels, but as one remembers"), then it must concentrate the vague remoteness of memory into the starry essence of a pure moment, which is no longer real and which is not fictive (and Joubert says: "My memory holds no more than the essence of what I read, of what I see and even of what I think"). A metamorphosis that he cannot hasten by the pressure of his will, for it does not depend on that authoritarian ego; it must, rather, unburden and eviscerate that ego, so that within it the unique contact can take place between the intimacy of the outside and the space of the inside. And so Joubert is waiting there, waiting for time to effect the passage to space, and waiting also for time to concentrate space into a pure essential moment, into the drop of light that will become a word and that, in the closed transparency of the word, will gather in one single utterance the whole expanse of all language.* A waiting which, at the same time, he must not dissociate himself from, which he must cooperate with by an interior work in which his whole life participates and, even more, by a great intimacy with words, since it is perhaps in words—the limit of time

---

*"Tormented by the cursed ambition always to put a whole book in a page, a whole page in a sentence and this sentence in a word. I am speaking of myself."

and space—that we can most properly take action, here, as he says
profoundly, where "there is . . . at once power and impossibil-
ity."

Repose in Light

If Joubert did not give up anything that seemed necessary to him,
it is still true that he was able to interpret this situation in such a
way that in the end he could find wisdom, calm, and perhaps appeasement in it. Here, he followed the inclination of his chilly genius without really disturbing the direction of his pursuit. When
he writes: "The revolution chased my mind from the real world
by making the world too horrible for me" (he was at first a revolutionary—though not an extremist—and an atheist—though
without a crisis of conscience), he is also pointing out the reason
he has always sought to establish between himself and things a
"zone of acceptance" "through which everything passes, sub-
sides, slows down, becomes tranquil, and lays aside its own ex-
cesses." And so he no longer exposes himself to separation and
distance as though to a painful demand, but so that he may make
for himself an "enclosure" that protects him, a quiet that "quilts
the ramparts," "an alcove," a defense "to absorb the shocks" and
"give the heart repose." Repose—that word kept him company
all his life. As a revolutionary, he seeks repose in negation. To
Mme de Beaumont, he says: "Find repose in love, in veneration."
Then the great theme he will devote his thought to is this: "Repose in light." He formulated it at the beginning of the Notebooks.
He says it at the end and sometimes repeats it day after day as
though it were a prayer or a magic formula: "(Burning. Burning
pains). Wisdom is repose in light" (October 22, 1821). October
24: "And for the last time, I hope. Wisdom is repose in light."
Why this obsessive recurrence? The reason is that here, in the
density of few words, the two inclinations of his thought are
recovered, and also the ambiguity of one thought with two inclinations, for repose in light can be—tends to be—peace through
light, light that appeases and that gives peace; but repose in light

is also repose—deprivation of all external help and impetus—so that nothing comes to disturb, or to pacify, the pure movement of light.*

The need for light, the great need for the day, for that spacious opening that is the day ("Without space, a point of light") and for that single point of brightness that makes the day and yields the day ("Luminous point. To seek it in everything. It is always in only one word in a phrase, in one idea in a discourse").

Aversion for everything that is obscure, impenetrable, opaque: "A dark point in his mind is as unbearable to him as a grain of sand in his eye." "Narrow? Yes, that part of my head is very narrow which is destined to receive things that are not clear." Too narrow, perhaps, for it is this distancing of darkness that also makes him turn away from the day, from what is too vivid in the early day; as he will say in a revealing thought, he prefers the twilight: "The twilight is charming, for it is a day that has been husbanded and diminished. But the dawn is less charming, for it is not yet a day. It is still only a beginning, or, as we say so rightly, it is the 'break,' the break of day." What he wants is "a middle light," and he dwells on the expression to confirm his taste for measure, but he also seeks to explore it more deeply, calling the light "middle" not only because it is measured, but because we always lack half of it: it is divided light and it is light that divides us, so that our contentment must be situated in this painful division of ourselves.

Repose in light: is it sweet appeasement through light? Is it the difficult deprivation of oneself and of all of one's own movement, a position in the light without repose? Here two infinitely different experiences are separated by almost nothing. Joubert remains important to us because he reminds us, by his special example, how essential it is, but also how difficult it is, to maintain this *nothing* that separates thought.

Maurice Blanchot
Translated by Lydia Davis

---

*". . . Repose is no small thing for it [the soul]. It represents a state in which [the soul] is subject only to its own movement without any foreign impetus."

Design by David Bullen
Typeset in Mergenthaler Bembo
by Wilsted & Taylor
Printed by Thomson-Shore
on acid-free paper